Rogue

L.M. Mountford

Edited by readabit: Copy Editing and Proofreading Services Est 2018
L.M. Mountford — 1st Ed.
ISBN: 978-1-913945-91-6

About the Author

L.M. Mountford's goal in life is to be unique, a character who stands out from the crowd that you just can't help remembering with a bemused chuckle.
A born and bred country boy from the southwest of England, he knew from an early age that he wanted to write and spent most of his time writing story ideas or playing Star Wars on his PlayStation.
Not much has changed over the years, though his stories have grown decidedly dirtier, and he swapped the Star Wars for Call of Duty.
Dubbed the Lord of Lust in 2019 and a firm believer that nothing sells like sex and violence, he loves writing about hard and gritty romantic thrillers, loaded with action men, sassy heroines, and a whole lot of dirty, sexy heat.

Bibliography

For a complete reading list, visit
LMMountford.com/bibliography/

Collections
Deliciously Sinful Liaisons
Sweet Temptations Box Set
Romancing the Tropics
Just a Number
Alpha Men of the Otherworld
Rogue Warrior
Rogue
The Sweet Temptations Series
The Babysitter
The Boss's Daughter
Just Friends Series
Just Once
Broken Heart Series
Broken
Tropical Cocktail Romance
Tequila Sunset
Beneath the Sheets
Confessions of a Trophy Wife
Forbidden Desire
Stand-alone Titles
Uncovered
Serving the Senator
Reckless
Training Tracey

THE LORD OF LUST

L.M. MOUNTFORD

Rogue

Rogue Warrior
A Tarzan Retelling
Book 1

THE LORD OF LUST PUBLICATIONS

Prologue

"Can you believe the balls on that Russki bastard?" I muttered, ejecting the mag of my Colt 1911. "Demanding a meeting after that stunt he pulled on Fifth Avenue." Satisfying myself it was still loaded, I slammed the mag back into place and worked the slider, chambering a round. "And on the night before your sister's wedding. God, we must be thick and fruity for going along with this."

"Like we had a choice…" Beside me, Turk watched the lights of New York City's nightscape streak past the tinted windows of the Maserati

Quattroporte. "The other families might line up to kiss our ass now. But you know as well as I do, the moment that *Bratva brutto figlio di puttana bastardo* gives the word, they'll be fighting each other for the honour of handing him our balls just to avoid another war. We can't fight both them and the Russians, not now, not while Pa is still in the hospital." His darkly handsome face was as impassive as ever, but his fingers rapped atop the arm rest, stirring up a beat that would have had Fred and Ginger foxtrotting from dusk till dawn. "We got lucky at the Tower, but Alexi's got everything he needs to destroy our family, and he knows it."

It was a shit poor speech, but all things considered, he'd hit the nail on the head. I couldn't blame him for being nervous.

He had called it the way it was. The Russians had our balls in a vice.

Hell, I had checked my piece twice already since getting into the back of the Maserati, and I had to resist the urge to check it again.

"Lucky?" I snorted, a dour smirk pulling at the corner of my mouth. "If I hadn't needed that piss when I did, we'd all have caught a bullet, instead of a cab."

I shoved the colt back into the holster of my shoulder rig concealed beneath my jacket, out of sight of any nosy pain-in-the-ass civilian that might happen across us. In the pocket under my right, there were two additional magazines.

At the first hint of trouble, I'd empty them all into Alexi's chops.

Who cares if it would start another gang war?

We've all gotta die someday. If my choice was today or later, better to shoot first in a cluster fuck of a parley, then end up another pussy, feeding fish on the bottom of the East River tomorrow morning.

Bloody Bratva bastards wouldn't catch me with my trousers down again.

Turk must have sensed what I was thinking because he turned and glowered at me. "Yeah, talk about a lucky shake." For all his usual jocular humour, his grin did not meet his eyes. "Look, I know your feelings about the man. After what his dog did to your family, well, no one could blame you for not liking the idea, but it's over. The war is over. You killed Tsabor. You've had your revenge, and now that the Scavos are dealt with, you've cemented your place in the family. We just need to keep the Russians sweet until Pa's well again. Then we'll settle old debts. We'll have our day, brother, I promise you that, but we need to be patient for now."

He was right, of course.

Say what you will about Turk DeCampo, and in my role of adopted little brother I often had, but he was rarely wrong.

It was one of the many things that made him so like his father.

They shared the same keen intellect, wily cunning, and infallible instinct, as well as that terrible low, slow burning fury that made them such terrible enemies. I had never seen either get angry. They never lost control. Their responses were always perfect. When I went all out, seeing red and wildly swinging a hammer, they stepped in with a nail straight to the target's heart.

None had contested his ascension to acting head of the family while Pa was recuperating in his hospital bed. He was the perfect choice. It was what he'd spent his life training for. He was a proven commander, had the loyalty of the men, and was respected, but feared by his enemies.

And then, of course, he also had me watching his back. The DeCampo's dreaded white ape enforcer. The orphan they had adopted from the streets and turned into their terrible pet Tarzan.

And like any good pet, I knew when to bow my head and wait for the master to scratch behind my ears. "If you say so."

G-force kicked like a mule as the driver dragged the wheel around at speed. With a squeal of tyres, the Maserati swerved off the 278 Interstate and down into the warren of dated apartment blocks and department stores fronted with graffitied tin shutters that made up lower Williamsburg.

Throw in a shot of Jennifer Aniston and Courtney Cox walking down the street and it could have been a city street scene ripped right out of Friends.

It was a joke. Developers had invested millions into Williamsburg over the past thirty years, attempting to gentrify the old neighbourhood. I guess whatever part they had allocated for this stretch of *Little Berlin* got lost enroute, and into the pocket of whichever *understanding* city examiner had the job of ensuring the work followed building regulations. It was amazing how much a keen-eyed examiner could put away for themselves. Then of course, there were union payoffs, supply and labour issues, and even the occasional under the counter deal with whatever politician or activist was arguing for the preservation of the community spirit.

The money men routinely factored such bribes into their sums, along with their commissions for handling such delicate matters.

That was all on top of the big piece of cheese the developers were pocketing for themselves.

Honestly, I'm amazed they ever even bothered building anything at all.

It was a legal crime. Money changed hands, growing smaller and smaller every time, until the well ran dry. Everybody knew and nobody cared, so long as the rich got richer, and they left these poor sods no worse off than they had been before.

Ingenious, and they called us the Mafia.

Hell, we weren't even in the same league. At least we had the courtesy to let someone know when they were getting fucked over.

The Naval Cemetery landscape was the one major beauty spot in the district. An area of the waterfront that had once been the site of the old Naval Hospital Cemetery until they had decommissioned it in the 1920s. A century on, and the city had given the site over to native Flora as a gift to the citizens, an escape from the urban jungle. That was how the politicians had sold it. Then they went and gave themselves a pat on the back, for figuring out a way to milk the taxpayer yet again. Minimum building or maintenance costs, but they could charge top dollar on venues for new age medicine nuts.

And I think they even got a commendation from greenpeace, as well as a mention in their newsletter.

Just goes to show, everyone's on the take in this game.

As we drove by, my eyes immediately moved to the darkness beyond where our destiny awaited. "Speaking of our time, whose bright fucking idea was it to hold this little *tête-à-tête* on the docks? And at fucking midnight? Do we have Scorsese and Hitchcock's ghost on the payroll now or something?

It's so unoriginal we might as well be selling tickets. Why not just turn up in a limo doing Marlon Brando impressions, and promise to make him an offer he can't refuse?"

"Well, no one ever accused the Russians of being creative," Turk agreed, pulling a monogrammed silver flask from his jacket pocket, unscrewing the lid, and chucking back a quick swig. "Besides, this isn't about originality, little brother. This is about making us feel safe. The docks are neutral ground, which makes it that much harder for either side to set up any surprises." He offered me the flask.

I waved it away.

"Yeah? That's what we thought last time," I said and fixed Turk with a deadly serious look. "You know what the definition for someone who keeps falling for the same trick but expects a different result every time is?"

"What? Insane?" he grinned, mocking me as he returned the flask to his pocket.

"No, a stupid fucking cunt." I forced a grim smile.

Turk's smile dropped, clearly having had enough of my bitching. "Oh, would you give it a rest already! You're making my ass ache."

I stiffened inwardly at the rebuke, unused to hearing that sharp tone directed my way. It was another thing that he and Pa had in common. They had the voice of commanders, able to turn from joking to furious in a moment, to quell a foe or raise a storm with just a few syllables.

"You're supposed to be my head of security, act like it," Turk continued, turning his attention back to his window. "Just focus on getting us through this in one piece and leave the thinking to me."

I nodded. "You're the boss, but…" I hesitated at a sharp look from him. I'd rarely experienced the sharper side of him myself. When he spoke to me, it was always like my big brother. He rarely snapped at me like I was a stray dog. All the others did, but never him. And yet, I knew I needed to carry on. My job was to keep him safe. How could I do that by letting him walk blindly into an obvious trap? I just needed to pick my words carefully. Turk didn't tell people twice. Not if they wanted to live, anyway. "But this just doesn't feel right."

Actually, it stank worse than a blocked New Delhi sewer drain in the middle of a heat wave. Unfortunately, I rather doubt the colourful, if not exactly exaggerated, turn of phrase would do me any favours.

"Well, get over it," he growled, yet even as he said it Turk couldn't look me in the eye. Not even when he added, "trust me."

I did. That went without question. There was no man I trusted more. He'd found me, pulled me out of the gutter and taken me home, vouched for me, protected me. I owed him everything, but I just couldn't shake the feeling we were about to walk into a serious cluster fuck.

Did he feel it too? That gut feeling you develop fighting through the scum and shit, the tingling on the back of the neck warning you something wasn't right. Or was there more? Did he know something I didn't?

I nodded all the same, just for show.

He turned back in his seat so his eyes were front and centre, and sure enough, we were pulling up to the gates of the Brooklyn Navy Yard.

The wrought iron bars stood open and unguarded, the security box just to the side empty as we drove through. A body lay in the cubicle, white and stiff on the floor in a pool of blood that wept out from a red smile that yawned wide beneath his jugular. That was the Bratva custom.

Cash could buy a man's silence for a time, but blood was always a certain insurance against careless gossip.

But bodies were messy things, and innocent civilians left such a stain on the floor. They were more difficult to clean up, and then there was always the chance he would have a family who would look for him wanting answers. How many unsolved crimes were there in this city? How many families were waiting for answers? Sooner or later, the count would be too high for the world to ignore and a politician would decide public opinion would do more for his career than dirty bribes under the table.

Then no price would buy his complicity and he would need to be made an example of.

And then the public would have another martyr, another rallying symbol for anyone with more balls than sense, like my parents.

Then it would just be a matter of time.

Ours was a dirty world, but there had to be balance.

Without balance, it was just a waiting game for that one missing person, the one that had been warned to stay away but didn't or was just in the wrong place at the wrong time, became one too many. Then the wheel would break, the ladder we were all fighting each other to climb would shatter, and it would all come crashing down on top of us.

So long as scum like the Bratva could do as they wished, our days would forever be numbered. One day, they would need to be taught a lesson, but Turk was right. Tonight, we couldn't win a war with them and the rest of the families.

The war had left our regime decimated. And even while we were playing for peace, the other families were greedily plundering much of what remained of the Scavo's forces. There would be more blood to come before long.

So tonight, we would be obedient.

Tonight, we were humble.

But our day would come...

"They're early."

The sleek black Sikorsky S-76C helicopter sat on the helipad at the end of the pier as we drove along the vast dry dock. The rotors were still and unmoving, the engine probably well on its way to freezing its bloody arse in the cold New York winter.

"Or we're late," Turk suggested.

"Fashionably so," I agreed grimly, my mouth set into a thin line.

It would have been bad manners to suggest anything else on such an occasion.

Turk shot me a look, but didn't bother with a rebuke as the Maserati Quattroporte came to a stop. Not waiting for the driver to kill the engine, he got out and slammed the door behind him. I followed quickly, stepping out into a cold gust of night wind that howled in my ears and made my eyes burn as I fell into line behind him.

Behind us, I heard two more car doors open and slam shut in the wind as Turk's driver, Joey Willisono and his mate Cassio Sforza, made up our rear. They would be our only back up tonight.

That had been the terms of the meeting. Just Turk, myself, and two guards. That was all. It sounded like a shit idea to me, but then what part of this plan hadn't?

Even the locale was a shit choice.

Buildings and warehouses surrounded us with windows on every level, clear overlapping fields of fire, no natural cover or alternative escape routes. Neutral ground my arse. A couple of snipers could cut us to swiss cheese. They couldn't have picked a better spot for an ambush.

We were walking into a goddamn kill box.

I suppose I should have just been grateful they hadn't made us come here with just our dicks in our hands. If it did all go to shit, at least we had a chance of shooting our way back to the car.

For what it was worth, I glanced right and left as we walked, eyes peeled, searching the overlooking windows, ready to act at the first hint of movement. That was my job, to watch his back. It was only on a shiver of instinct I glanced back the way we came, and felt my blood turn to ice in my veins.

"Where's Joey and Cassio?" I hissed at Turk, leaning in close so we couldn't be overheard.

"Sick," he answered simply, not looking back or offering anything more.

Sick? I chewed on the explanation incredulously, but knew better than to press him. "So you called in Lucca and Anthony?"

"Don't worry about it, they're good," his voice crackled with undisguised irritation and he picked up the pace, lengthening the gap between us. I knew I should have pressed it, but I let him go. I was *his* head of security. If there was a problem with his guard detail, it was my problem, my responsibility, and my fuck up. I should have checked before getting in the car, but they'd pulled up and everything had happened so fast, I got in without thinking.

Now it was too late.

I'd fucked up. Nothing to do now but roll with it and hope it wouldn't come back to bite me in the arse.

I glanced back again. Lucca Zaboni and Anthony Clamenza. Yeah, not exactly my first choice of reserves.

Actually, they'd never have even made the list.

Cassio and Joey knew their jobs. I could trust them to keep their heads down and just focus on getting Turk in the car. Lucca and Anthony however…

Don't get me wrong, they were good. Good big lads. Proper Sicilian soldiers. Aggressive and hard, good street fighters, just the sort you'd want for intimidating store owners or putting the frighteners to witnesses. They were also as thick as two short planks and greener than grass. They could follow orders well enough but had all the initiative of a rock and took to thinking like a duck to a dog track. If it did all go to hell tonight, they were as likely to spray the street with lead as they were to hit their marks.

On the helipad, the doors to the Sikorsky slid open and a set of steps unfolded smoothly into place. On either side, two heavies jumped down into a flanking position. The typical Russian greeting. They were all muscle, leather, and biker tattoos. Both had hard looks. One was near bald, with a face like a constipated bulldog who'd mistaken a rope of barbed wire for its chew toy. The other had short, cropped, bleached blonde hair and looked like a bull that had just had some good news from a butcher's tenderiser.

Yet they weren't the ones making my fingers twitch.

That was the old bastard between them, making his way down the small flight of steps and across the helipad towards us.

Their boss. The Pakhan. Alexi Lebedinsky. An exiled oligarch and arguably the most powerful man in New York, perhaps the country.

And the man who had ordered my family's murder.

We stopped just short of halfway, at the foot of a rusty old platform that bridged the gap between the dock and the helipad, just ten metres between us and them. Ten metres between me and the revenge I had so longed for.

My fingers were twitching so badly I might have looked like I was having a stroke. Trying to force down the urge, I clenched my fist and shoved it in my pocket.

Bulldog noticed and thumbed back the front of his jacket to show the grip of the revolver shoved into his belt.

A big one.

Powerful, but heavy. Very heavy.

Too heavy to be quick on the draw.

A dumbass gun to bring to a shootout.

The sort that would have Dirty Harry sporting morning wood at midnight.

Turk cleared his throat. "Hey there Alexi, how've you been? Sorry we're a bit late. Traffic was a dog."

"Late?" Alexi's lips pressed into a pale thin line. "No, I think not. I'm afraid we're early."

He was a straight man. Not big, but straight and as sharp as a blade in his impeccably tailored grey suit, with a long face cut with deep long lines and framed by shoulder length black hair. He might have looked like a wall street executive, if not for his eyes. They were cold and hard, like a chunk of black ice in each socket, and completely unreadable.

They suited his reputation well enough, like the blow torch, hammer and DeWalt drill set he probably kept hidden away in the boot of that chopper.

Turk just bowed his head respectfully. "If you say so." What else could he say?

"Good." The line across Alexi's face twisted in a cruel parody of a smile, then his eyes shifted to take in our party. "You've brought what I asked?"

What? Was there a change of plan? And since when were we the Bratva's delivery boys?

I glanced at Turk, but his eyes remained firmly fixed on Alexi. "Yes."

The old bastard nodded, suddenly looking very smug. "Then I guess we have a deal."

"I guess we do," my brother growled.

"Now don't be like that, boy. You should be pleased. With this one sacrifice, you've secured your family's future. But perhaps I misjudged you?" He spread his arms out, palms open in expectation, as exaggerated as that fucking accent. "Perhaps this task is too much for you and now you're having misgivings. *Perhaps* you'd prefer to go back on our little deal."

The question hung in the air between them.

Yet even as time held its breath, I couldn't shake the feeling that had been tying my guts into knots. What the fuck was going on?

Instinct shivered through me and I glanced at the Bulldog and his mate. Both were watching me.

"No," Turk growled, then turned to me. "I'm sorry." He still couldn't meet my eyes, instead they were looking at something behind me. He dipped his head in a small nod. "Take him."

I didn't have time to ask what he meant.

Behind us, the night rang with a dull thud and click. Recognising the sound of a hammer being primed, I pivoted, moving to put myself between Turk and the threat at our back, one hand going for the 1911-

Only Lucca Zaboni and Anthony Clamenza already had their guns out and on me.

Chapter One

Washington State was beautiful in Autumn.

The weather was fucking awful, but it was still beautiful.

Beneath the thick canopy of grey storm clouds, the forests of the Olympic Peninsula's northern slopes were a riot of colour. A wondrous collage of yellows, reds and oranges, amidst a sea of lush green that was all the more vivid amidst the gloom of an impending downpour. In the morning, the air was alive with birdsong, while the evenings rang to the haunting chorus of the Roosevelt Elk that grazed across the land.

Unfortunately, now there was only the roar of the Chevrolet Suburban's engine as it navigated up the winding dirt road.

I watched it come from the rocking chair on my balcony, hoping they were just some thick-as-shit ramblers that had got themselves lost on the Clallam Bay Trail, but I wasn't that hopeful. The trail started a good 10 miles down the Strait of Juan de Fuca Highway, in the so-named town, and never left the highway.

Even Ray Charles couldn't miss the signs.

Then again, I didn't have visitors.

You don't go through the hassle of leasing land on the Makah reservation if you want a roaring social life.

The Tribal Council's price was extortionate, but it was worth it. No visitors. No nosy neighbours. Not even the odd Jehovah's Witness trying his luck with the *'heathens'*.

The community and I had an understanding. If I left them alone, they'd leave me alone. Apart from my occasional trip up to Neah Bay for supplies, they had practically no idea I even existed. Which worked just fine for me.

Which begged the question, whose SUV was that driving up my driveway?

Well, there was only one way to find out. Maybe they were just going to ask for directions. They clearly couldn't read. I'd put up Private property signs everywhere.

I met them at the door just as the Grey Suburban pulled up. The passenger door opened, and King Kong, dressed in a poor fitting black suit and shades, stepped out. One look had my mind jumping to the Remington 870 12Gauge and the SIG 9mm in my weapons locker, just out of sight of the barn doors and just out of reach.

Then the Driver's door opened and this time Donkey Kong stepped out, done up in a matching costume. Maybe Ray-Ban had a two for one sale on. Then he stepped round to open the back door, and King Louie stepped down. Middle-aged and smaller, but dressed in a much nicer suit than his pair of gorillas, this guy was clearly the money.

No shades though, maybe Ray-Ban didn't have something to go with the Harris Tweed. Probably for the best. Sunglasses would suit that pudgy face and bald pate encircled by tufts of curly ginger hair about as well as tits on a bull.

"Mr Greystoke?"

He said my name without a stutter, but his voice trembled all the same beneath that smooth, business-like manner. He was nervous.

Good, he should be. I didn't like uninvited guests.

I ignored his question, and his minders, and looked him dead in the eye. "If you're lost, the highway is back that way, past the keep out signs."

His sallow face dropped, his business-like mask faltering slightly as he licked his lips, but he kept on. "Ah, no, no we're not lost, Mr Greystoke." He extended his hand, a bold gold signet ring dressing one chubby sausage finger. "My name is Ritter, Jiles Ritter, and I have some business to discuss with you."

I glared at him until the hand dropped back to his side. "Well, I don't want any, and I'm not buying."

"I'm not here to sell you anything, Mr Greystoke. I'm buying."

"Well, I'm not selling." Bored with conversation, I turned to head back inside. "Be sure to use a low gear when the track goes down the hill or your brakes will go."

Out of the corner of my eye, I glimpsed Donkey Kong stepping forward, no doubt having half a mind, in more than one sense, to stop me. I steeled myself to put the Gorilla down, knowing I'd need to do it fast, before King Kong could join in. But then Ritter got a word in first. "Mrs Bourne recommended you. Says you're just the sort of man I'm looking for."

I paused mid-step and threw a curious look back. "Elvira Bourne?" I waited for him to bite. It was easy to pick a name out of a glossy magazine full of the rich and famous. In my line, I could have worked for any of them.

He looked confused for a moment, as if trying to place the name, then embarrassedly corrected me. "Err… Elizabeth, and her ex-husband."

Ahhh… now it all made sense. Mrs Elizabeth Bourne, or rather Crane, as she now was. She'd needed my help a few months ago persuading her *philanthropist* husband, who was to music what Harvey Weinstein was to films, to give her a divorce. An easy enough task in itself, but not, however, when you considered the ironclad prenup, the young and then lovesick, soon to be Mrs Bourne had signed without a second thought. She'd needed a way around it.

The terms were simple enough. The then Mrs Elizabeth Bourne got nothing unless her husband did something stupid and got it splashed all over the tabloids. Scandal and humiliation were the cancer of the rich and famous. It had been my pleasure to facilitate it, with the help of two call girls with dreams of being photographers, a farmer, or rather a few of his barnyard pigs, and a healthy but non-threatening dose of drugs that would put Mr Bourne out like a light, and hard as a rock.

No doubt the newly single, and very grateful, Mis Crane had recommended me after hearing about whatever trouble this guy had got himself into.

"Come inside." I was about to lead him in, then paused, thought better of it, and glanced back over my shoulder. "Just you, the Gorillas stay outside."

I'd read somewhere that the land had once belonged to a horse rancher who'd bought it from the tribal council in 1922. Unfortunately, the market crash of 29 hit his interests hard and while drowning his sorrows, he managed to set fire to the main house while he was passed out inside it. In the years that followed, the ground remained unused until the Tribal council finally won their legal battle to have the land returned to them in 1994, when all traces of the main house's gutted structure were gone.

Somehow untouched in the fire, the barn had survived, more or less, and the council had converted the rafters into an open plan studio flat. The ground level remained much as it had back in the good old days, a large, open space, with a row of stalls along the back wall. My land cruiser sat in the one on the end, undercover and in dire need of servicing. Behind it, the diesel generator coughed and sputtered like a smoker on fifty-a-day in its cupboard.

I avoided the stairs leading to the flat and circled the old rustic desk with a frayed dark green leather topper that took up the centre of the space to sit in the chair. Ritter remained standing. There wasn't a second chair, and I didn't intend to offer him one.

Outside, the gorillas waited by the car. I ignored them and fixed my gaze on the small man.

"Right," I barked. "So, first things fucking last, Mr Ritter, never come to my place unannounced again. You want to see me, you make an appointment like everyone else, got it?"

"Yes," he nodded, his head bobbing in a way that made him look a bit like a penguin.

Having established that one important fact, I relaxed back into my chair and steepled my fingers together. "So, what's this business?"

"Well, you see Mr Greystoke… err," he seemed torn between relief and nervousness. "I'm not quite sure how to say this, this isn't exactly the sort of thing I'm accustomed to."

Feeling the tale-tale throbbing of a headache starting, I resist the urge to massage my temples, already regretting the decision to hear him out. "Well, just start from the beginning, Mr Ritter, and see where that goes. You'll probably find it gets easier as you go on."

"Well, it's just that it's been months now, and they haven't paid me back, not a cent. I can't wait any longer."

"You owe money?" I ask, my interest peaked. This guy certainly didn't look the sort that shopped at Good Will and Oxfam. Unless they'd opened up a branch on Savile Row in the last month and the story hadn't broken yet.

He paled at the suggestion. "No, it's my partner. He's very displeased. It wasn't his money, you understand, but he says that outstanding debts owed to our consortium, even if it's only on paper, are bad for business. He thinks it makes him look weak, by association."

A partner?

The idea intrigued me.

Sounded like Mr Ritter had wanted to swim with the big boys but instead found himself in the shark tank and was just managing to hold his head above water.

"So why come to me? You've got lawyers. Let the courts handle this."

"That would take too long," he spluttered, sweat misting his forehead. "Please, Mr Greystoke. I need the money back by Friday evening, before the banks close."

I checked my watch. It was Monday, a little after nine in the morning. Not a lot of time then. Difficult, but not impossible. There was a clunk outside, and my eyes darted to the door. The minders must have got bored because they'd started fishing around inside the SUV. "Well, what about your two friends out there? They're big lads. They should be able to handle this for you."

"Oh No, Mark and Luke, no, no, no, that wouldn't
do at all. I'm a well-known man, Mr Greystoke. I have
friends, business associates, and they know their
faces. If something went wrong and word got out, it
would all come back to me. Any hint of violence or
criminal activity would ruin me."

I resisted the impulse to ask which one was Luke
and which was Mark. They looked pretty much
identical to me. With their broad barrel builds and
sloping temples, Donkey and King suited them much
better.

"But you do want your money, right?" My
headache was growing, and this time I couldn't help
but rub my temples. Never mind minders, this guy
needed a fucking nanny.

"I need it, Mr Greystoke, by Friday." And the look
on his face was so desperate, I thought he might drop
to one knee and start kissing my arse.

"Very well, just write down their names and
addresses, the amounts they owe, and how long for."
I pulled out a pad of writing paper and a pen from
the desk draw, slapped them down on the topper and
slid them over to him.

He did so, in a scribble so quick it was only just
legible, then slid it back to me. "There, please, Mr
Greystoke, I can't wait any longer."

I looked them over. Three names. All relatively
local, not considerable sums, though the amount for

number three meant he might be a problem. That one would definitely need some convincing, maybe a bit of arm twisting… or breaking.

Hopefully, it wouldn't go that far, but you never knew.

I looked Ritter in the eye, letting him know I was deadly serious. "I'll get you your money, Mr Ritter, don't worry, but this isn't a charity. My fee is fifteen percent, plus expenses, understand?"

"Of course, don't worry, you'll have it. Just hurry, please."

I nodded in understanding.

And with that, we were done. He turned and hurried out of the barn, back to the SUV.

I watched them drive away from my chair until the Suburban was out of sight. My phone vibrated in my pocket. Unlocking the screen with my fingerprint, it came alive to show a camera's live feed. It was motion-sensitive, one of several I'd rigged up all around the ground. The SUV moved into screen and two symbols appeared at the bottom, red circles with the legend *BOOM*.

My thumb hovered over one, and it sorely tempted me to blow Mr Rigger and the Kong brothers straight to hell for a moment. God, it would be so easy.

Instead, I closed the app and opened up the web browser.

Within a few clicks, I'd learned almost everything there was to know about Jiles Ritter. It was boring stuff.

Unmarried. No kids. A financier of various small-scale businesses and organisations, all legitimate. So, what sort of partner could he have that would make him so nervous?

Satisfied but curious, I put my phone on the table and went upstairs to get dressed into something more suitable.

I had work to do.

And what fun it would be.

No violence. I laughed out loud at that. Mr Ritter clearly lived in a comfy little padded cell, or just in Never Never Land. Just how did he expect me to get his money back in a few days without banging a few heads together? Yell trick-or-treat at them?

Money lending was a dirty business. When the debts went unpaid, that didn't leave many avenues for collection.

Outside, the rains began.

It was still pissing it down when I stepped out of the Uber car. The driver, a heavy Hispanic who'd looked rather like a young Antonio Banderas, but wore a badge that said his name was Earl, had picked me up from a quiet little layby on the highway. For the first five minutes of the trip, he'd complained bitterly about having to come so far out. Then when he read the destination, he gave me a double helping of grief that, rather than going back towards civilization, I wanted, as he put it, to be taken even further into the arse end of nowhere. He probably couldn't understand why I even needed an Uber, rather than drive myself.

Apparently, out here, everyone had a car of their own. It was the American way, so why the fuck didn't I get with the program?

Well, fuck him. I had my reasons, and they were none of his business.

Slamming the door on any more of the Earl's whining, I started up the dirt slip road, hard-packed by the constant traffic of HGVs and machinery. It snaked for about half a mile. The overhanging canopy kept most of the downpour off, but it was a treacherous trek all the same. More than once I had to catch myself before my boots slipped out from underneath me and sent me sprawling face-first into the shit and mud.

A clap of thunder boomed, mingling with the splatter of falling raindrops and the rumble of engines as a steady procession of Wagons, SUVs and Trucks started driving by. A quick check of my watch showed that it was nearly half twelve, lunchtime. Good, that would make things easier. Between rants. my new best mate Earl had gone on about a dinner somewhere down the highway, The Bear's Den Dinner, just past the boundary of the reservation, that boasted the best burgers in the state. These boys were probably all on their way to put the boast to the test. I just hoped they weren't in the mood for the lunch time special. Earl said the fries were grizzly.

After about twenty paces, the canopy opened, and I walked out into a clearing and spotted my target.

The first name on the list was the easiest to find. Hell, we were as good as neighbours after all.

Jasper Christopher Delvacio, a logger, or rather, the owner of the JCD Lumber company. His family had been Logger Barons, but Jasper had quickly lost the family fortune as public opinion switched from fossil fuels to more environmentally conscious, sustainable methods. Or rather preferred to look the other way and play ignorant while enjoying the benefits of the third world destroying their forests and woodland to feed western greed, at rock-bottom prices.

From everything to nothing in no time at all.

He'd gone from being the heir of a timber empire to being in debt to Mr Ritter, and no doubt even more angry creditors were waiting in the wings.

I didn't need to wonder where the bulk of his money had gone.

Every few years, the Tribal council would auction off leases for woodland that had become overgrown to the logging companies. It was a beautiful system, really. The loggers were desperate for lumber to chop down, and the Tribal Council needed land cleared. The loggers bid for the rights to cut down the trees, then when the leases were up, the council got the rights to the land back and whatever land they didn't need got returned to nature. Better yet, it was all done on the loggers' dime with no bleeding-hearts screaming about the exploitation of the natives.

Jasper had claimed the rights to three leases with outrageously high bids that had made the local headlines. It had been quite a picture-op. The local businessman standing shoulder to shoulder with the Tribal Council Members outside the Council building, dressed in his tailored three-piece and presenting them a large novelty cheque from the boot of his flash new 911 Porsche.

He'd probably paid for the photoshoot on top of everything else.

No wonder Mr Ritter was having kittens.

It was the same old story. Struggling business executive, barely able to keep his head above water, throwing money around in an all front and bullshit show to make it look like he was anything but skint.

The 911 was certainly flash. Cherry red and polished to a high shine, it practically screamed money and suited the middle of a logging camp about as well as a Greenpeace van. But there it was, all the same. Sat there besides a mud-splattered mobile trailer office that, beneath its fresh coat of whitewash, had seen better days. Everything else was just as one would expect. Big machines arranged in a circle, rows of flatbed trucks waiting for loading, and huge lengths of timber piled high as far as the eye could see.

Business was obviously good.

I stopped by the 911 and took out my phone. A quick search of the *Seattle Auto Trader* lists told me everything I needed to know. Dropping the phone back into my jacket pocket, I was about to go up the trailer stairs when the door opened and Jasper Christopher Delvacio stepped out to welcome me with a broad grin and open arms.

Well, he stepped out to welcome me anyway, along with a welcome party of three lumberjacks. Complete with thick bushy beards and check flannel shirts, they could have been characters ripped right out of some old folktale.

I turned my eyes up to them, forced a pleasant smile, and did my best to ignore the rain running into my eyes. "Ahhh, you must be Mr Delvacio. I recognise you from your picture in The Post."

He didn't return my smile. "Yeah, that's me. Who wants to know?"

He'd ditched the three-piece for a simple grey two-piece that had seen a few too many winter days, and a plain white shirt that struggled to contain his barrel chest.

He crossed his arms. They weren't the sort of arms that belonged to a man who'd spent a lifetime earning with his hands. It wouldn't take much to break this man, I decided. His friends, though, could be a problem.

My guess would be Jasper knew exactly how much shit he was in with his creditors and had taken steps against reprisals.

Well, in the words of Sid James, *Now gentlemen, this revolt will have to be suppressed with the utmost tact, and Diplomacy… we'll string up half a dozen of them for a start.*

"Now there's no need for that, Mr Delvacio. I have some business to discuss with you." Keeping my smile in place, I tried to sound friendly, nonthreatening. This would go a lot easier if I could get him to drop the guards and invite me inside.

Except it seemed Jasper wasn't in a mood to play nice. Keeping his arms crossed, he stared down at me with a look that said he wasn't buying anything. "Oh really, aren't you a little small for a woodcutter?"

I couldn't help but laugh at that. At five, ten, and a little under 200lbs, no one had ever called me small before. Well, except for my brother, of course, but then Turk had always been a gorilla. "Ah, no, no, you're right. I'm not a woodcutter, Mr Delvacio, but you and I do have a mutual friend. Mr Ritter. And it's him I need to talk to you about."

The smaller man's face visibly paled at the mention of the name, then twisted into a glare that I guess was supposed to be threatening, rather than constipated, "This is private property, you're trespassing."

"Oh, am I? Well, I'm sorry about that, Mr Delvacio, but you're a very naughty boy. You owe our mutual friend a considerable amount of money. What is it now, err…" I pulled Mr Ritter's list of names from my pocket and exaggerated a whistle. "$53,268, plus the agreed interest, which makes it an even sixty thousand dollars. And well, he wants what's owed."

If I'd been expecting any sort of reaction, I would have been disappointed. Rather, Jasper just looked bored by the news.

"Ah I see, you're a messenger boy," he sneered, then suddenly his face lightened and he let out a small laugh that held little humour. Maybe he'd had a few of these sorts of messages already. "Okay, so you've delivered the message and you can tell Ritter he'll get his money. Now my friends here will see you back to your car."

"Err…" Edging back, I did my best to look embarrassed and shoved the paper back into my jacket pocket as the three lumberjacks started down the steps towards me. "No, I'm not a messenger boy, Mr Delvacio. I'm a delivery boy. And I didn't bring a car."

They fanned out. The first moved to my right, the second to the left, half encircling me. They could have been twins, except the one on the right wore a traditional logger's fur hat with earflaps, while the other had a beanie.

The third, however, was the very walking embodiment of Paul Bunyan and came straight at me, driving me further back.

"Really, well that's a shame because it's a long walk back to town. You better watch yourself. There's a lot of dangerous animals here in the woods, you know. We lose guys every couple of months. Bears. Mountain Lions. They'll drag bodies into the woods and sometimes they're never found again. Best you go now before it gets dark. You might just make it back safe."

The threat was as clear as day.

Nice try, but two could play that game.

"Well, thank you for the warning, Mr Delvacio, but I think I better stay." Even as I said the words, I raised my hands defensively, passively, showing them I wasn't a threat as I backed away. "After all, if the animals got me and I never delivered your reply, well, who knows what could happen. Especially as you've got an awful lot of wood and machinery here, Mr Delvacio, and it's very dangerous, leaving it all piled up together like that. The two don't mix. This time of year, storms come and go like that." I clicked my fingers, and as if to prove my point, a bellow of thunder boomed overhead, right on cue. "One bolt of lightning, one little spark, and this whole place could go up in flames. Then you'd have nothing, and then how would you pay Mr Ritter what you owe him, hmmm?"

Jasper's smile was gone by the time I finished. He'd caught my meaning, recognised the threat. His answer was exactly what I'd expected. "Tom!"

Paul Bunyan, or apparently Tom, grinned and closed in. In a grizzled voice, he barked "Hey pal, Mr Delvacio said it's time for you to-"

He tried to grab me, one huge paw sweeping out, missing me by miles as I appeared to slip in the mud. I tumbled sideways, then pivoted beneath the arm, thick and bulging with solid muscle, to drive my fist into his ribs as I went.

He grunted with the pain and twisted to follow, that same huge arm swinging like an axe to chop me down, but I'd already danced back and out of range. My hands back up in the unthreatening pose like nothing had happened. "Oh I'm sorry, gentleman, you're making me very nervous, that's all."

Beanie and Fur Cap just looked from me to Tom, and then at each other, not sure what had just happened. Guess this wasn't going according to their script. They'd probably been taking odds on if I'd run away or just piss myself. That I'd fight back would never have even crossed their minds. Maybe they'd let me put a bet on it. The way things were looking right then, I'd be in for quite a windfall, if they're still able to walk after that is.

Except, it seemed Tom wouldn't give me the chance.

"Bastard," he snarled, his grin gone and rainwater rolling down his face into his beard. He'd be feeling the sucker punch, and it wouldn't have done anything to improve his disposition. Angry but confident, he charged bodily, like a bull at the run. He knew how to fight. He knew he was bigger and stronger. Those facts made him think he would win.

And that was his mistake.

Yes, he could fight. He would have had a lot of fights over the years. Drunken bar brawls late at night, where size and brute strength were all that mattered. Yes, he was bigger than me, and probably stronger. However, I doubt he'd ever fought someone like me before. While I'd been putting down big bastards like him all my life.

I wasn't strong, not like this guy, all muscle and brute force, but I was fast, fast and savage. That was how I'd survived my years on the streets of New York City. Down there, in the rat's nests, when the big guy walks up and tells you what he wants, you either put him down quickly, or you bend over and prepare for penetration.

And I wasn't into buggery.

So as he charged forward, I sidestepped again, twisting out of his path at the last moment. He carried on past me, too big and heavy to stop and react as I rugby tackled his flank and sent him skidding into the mud and shit. He went down hard, all that solid muscle suddenly working against him.

The bigger you are, as they say…

I would have finished him there and then, while I had the chance. Queensbury's rules were for public schoolboys on the playground. In the real world, a fight was dirty and to win, you had to play dirtier than all the rest. Unfortunately, Fur Cap and Beanie had finally taken stock and had joined the fray. They were both big lads, not quite so large as Tom, but faster. It was obvious why Jasper had got them to watch his back.

Beanie was closer and had one huge paw pulled back in a swing. Leaving the bigger man spluttering in the mud, I moved to meet him, my left raised, catching the inside of the swing before it could fall, my right arching up, elbow leading.

It had never ceased to amaze me how many people made the mistake of leading with a punch. Oh, a punch could lay a man out sure enough, but there were so many little bones in the hand, so many things that could snap or break if things went badly. The elbow, however, was a joint encased in a shell of solid bone that packed a hit like a solid iron mace, if used correctly.

Beneath the mess of his wild, bushy beard, my elbow met the man's jaw with a crack, snapping his head up and back. His body followed as his legs, still trying to run, skidded wildly in the mud. One hand snapped out as he fell, trying to grab me, but I'd already twisted away, just managing to duck under Beanie's attack.

The third woodcutter was faster still. No sooner had I avoided one meaty fist than the other was coming, glancing off my shoulder, driving me back another step. He followed, fists jabbing for my face, but punching only the rain as I weaved and ducked, then stepped in and answered by driving my knee into his crotch. He gasped and doubled over in pain, into the path of my fist that slammed into his jaw and sent him crashing to the ground. A hard kick ensured he'd stay down.

No sooner had I laid Beanie down, however, than something huge smashed down on my shoulder, numbing it to the bone. I wheeled with it and found Tom back on his feet, advancing on me, rain running down his mud splattered face. He grinned, a feral toothed grin, and a pair of huge arms suddenly enveloped me in a bear hug.

"You'll pay for that," Fur Hat growled wetly, hauling me back and off my feet and crushing me to his chest. The closeness made me want to gag. The guy really needed to invest in a few packs of extra strong TicTacs, and maybe a can or two of Lynx.

Desperate to escape the reek, I twisted and writhed like an eel, trying to drive my elbows into his ribs, or stamp my heels down on his feet. But the guy had a hold like an alligator wrestler. Then he started to squeeze, and I couldn't help grunting at the feeling of the arms tightening around me, constricting me like the coils of a great python.

Out of the corner of my eye, I saw Tom flexing his muscles like a boxer entering the ring, advancing on us. Knowing I had just seconds to break free, I arched and smashed my head back into the logger's face. Pain seared across my skull as it connected with something solid, but Fur Hat must have got the worst of it because he let out a roar and his hold loosened. It was only a slight release, but it was enough.

Trying to fight two opponents at once was a mug's game. They would always have the upper hand, be able to deal out twice as much damage while only taking half the punishment. The trick was to deal with them one at a time. Put down one quick, so you could then deal with the other. It wasn't a perfect system. It worked, most of the time, but at times like this, you just had to be a mug.

And take both men on at once.

I kicked out, smashing my heel into the side of Tom's knee. The big woodcutter roared in surprise and agony, his leg buckling. I pivoted as he went down, ripping my right arm free of Fur Cap's grip, and brought it round to hammer into his face. My elbow had turned his mouth into a red ruin, and my headbutt had taken care of his nose. He reeled with the force of the punch, but I followed as he went back, cranking my fist back to deliver another, and then another, until he toppled to the ground in a bloody mess. He wouldn't be getting up from that for a while.

There was a low wheezing sound coming from my back, and when I turned, I saw that Tom had curled himself into a ball and was clutching at his knee. "God damn, that hurts, doesn't it?" I asked, grinning. People always expected to get kicked in the balls.

They forgot there were other, far more effective targets. "If I were you, I'd just sit there for a while. Maybe you won't need crutches for the rest of your li-"

The axe was a big, two-handed chopper with a broad blade. I felt the wind of it brush against my face as it sliced by and lurched back as the weight of the axe carried Jasper past me. He'd definitely spent more time in the office than sweating out here in the wilds with the lads. His hands were too close together, and he handled it worse than Kate Winslet on Titanic.

He swung around to face me and brandished the axe like a sword, his eyes wide with a mix of fury and panic. Never a good mix for rational thinking.

"Oh yeah, very cute," I said, backing away another step, needing to put some distance between me and the axe. "Now put that thing down before you hurt yourself."

However, Jasper wasn't in any state of mind to listen. He'd been confident before, with three big guys watching his back, but they were all out of it now and he was alone, and he'd started flapping. He came after me as I edged back, bringing that axe up and around. I twisted so that it passed me by, but he was quicker to recover than I'd expected and brought it around again for another swing. I kicked as he did, driving the flat of my shoe into his unguarded belly, throwing him back into the mud. The axe flew from his hands and clattered to the ground between us.

"Now," I say, panting slightly as I pick up the axe and go to stand over him. "Wouldn't it be simpler just to pay our mutual friend what's owed? Huh?"

"I haven't got the money, alright," he groaned, his upper lip trembling, but his eyes fixed on the axe blade that hung over his throat. He was a pathetic sight, stretched across the filth in his grey suit, like a turtle on its back. My kick had left a smeared mud print across his soaked shirt, and I wasn't sure if the water running down his cheeks was rain, sweat, or tears. "I just need more time."

I smirked and chuckled. "Yeah, I thought you'd say something like that. Isn't it funny how many people recon they can pay off their debts, with just a more time. Well, unfortunately, Mr Ritter hasn't got the time. But I do have a solution." Reaching into my jacket's other pocket, I pulled one of the two identical sheets of paper that I'd printed off at the barn and handed them to him. "Here you go."

He took it cautiously. "What's this?"

"Well now, that's a receipt for that very flash car of yours over there. At current market value, that should more than cover your debt to Mr Ritter, as well as the interest owed and-"

"What!" He cut me off, his eyes going wide with disbelief as he looked from the document to me. Then outrage. "That's a 911 Turbo S cabriolet! It's mortgaged for over two hundred thousand dollars. I'm not selling it for sixty-Ahh!" His voice died away in a gurgle as I pressed my boot into the soft meat of his neck.

"Oh yes you are, Jasper, unless Mr Ritter gets his money by Friday morning. Now, sign, come on." My face was hard as I pressed down on his throat, just long enough for his eyes to go wide and have him clawing for breath. When I pull back slightly, he takes a pen from his jacket and scribbles a hasty signature on the dotted line, the last of his defiance gone. I check it, then fold and pocket it before handing him the other copy. "That's a good boy. Now there's your copy, my numbers on the bottom. You call me when you have the money and you'll get the car back. Until then, keys please." I extended my hand, but he was already fishing the fob from his pocket. Taking the card, I smiled pleasantly down at him. "Pleasure doing business with you, Mr Delvacio."

Turning my back on the broken group, I dropped the axe and walked to the Porsche. Unlocking it with a click of the fob, I slid into the driver's seat. It was the latest model, with all the optional extras included and a steering wheel like something on the Starship Enterprise. Fortunately, the keyless ignition button was easy to spot.

The engine roared to life, and Britney Spears started screeching through the speakers. It was fucking awful, but I didn't have time to figure out how to shut her up. Instead, I slid the car into drive and sped away without a backward look.

Chapter Two

The Beached Whale was the quintessential American dive bar and grill.

Rustic and rundown, it stood two miles outside the city limits of Port Angeles, within a glade looking out across the dark waters of Freshwater Bay.

The gravel of the not quite empty car park crunched under the 911's tires as I pulled off the dirt road and parked up outside the structure, near an old Ford F-150 pickup that might have been one of the first off the original line and hadn't moved since my first visit.

Having finally figured out how to silence Britney's caterwauling about a mile back, I killed the engine and climbed out the sports car into the cool afternoon air. The rain was holding off, and stray beams of sunlight had broken through the grey canopy. With any luck, it might help dry me out before the Porsche's upholstery became too waterlogged.

Pocketing the fob, I turned to walk inside, and couldn't help my grin.

Above the foyer, the green billboard that broadcasted the name of the establishment in red neon lights also sported a huge blue neon design hovering atop it. Presumably, whatever dip shit had put the rig together had thought it was a decent likeness of the bar's name's sake, a beached whale.

So far, only the drunkest of patrons had seen anything even slightly resembling a sea creature in the mess of blue. Personally, I thought it looked more like an inebriated hippopotamus.

The doors opened with a gust of warm air, fragrant with stale beer, fried food and cigarette smoke, and I walked right onto the set of True Blood.

With its wooden floors and walls, the Whale's interior was about as rustic as the exterior, though thankfully not quite so run down. There was a big oak bar and stools in one corner, backed by row upon row of vintage booze and spirits, but apart from that the rest of the open floor space had been given over to a dining area made up of a mix of booths and tables. A window where the staff could pass orders through to the kitchen dominated the rear wall. Two chalk boards hung on either side, listing the menu, Wi-Fi charges, and a sign asking the diners that, as the staff didn't eat out of their toilets, could they please not piss on the floor. That about set the tone of the place.

Off to the side, a set of swinging doors led out to a converted game room, complete with retro slot machines and a pool table. Inside, a group of guys were playing a game, loudly. I doubted anyone was likely to kick up much of a fuss, though. They were the Whale's only patrons at the moment, besides myself, and I sure as hell wasn't about to go back there to tell them to keep it down.

The barman -his staff badge had named him Mike- just nodded at me as I made for my usual seat, a booth halfway down the wall. I wasn't a frequent enough visitor to be considered a regular, but I'd frequented the place enough times for the staff to recognise me. Mike signalled to Debra, the only waitress on the clock at the moment, then returned to watching the tv in the top corner of the bar where the Seahawks were playing.

Debra was already waiting by my booth.

She was a pretty thing, a curvy redhead who wore a touch too much make-up but who greeted every customer with a ready smile that ensured she always got a good tip. "Well hi there, sugar pie, we don't often see you dropping by for the early bird special."

I grinned and pretended not to know she called every guy that came in alone *sugar pie*. "Aw well, you know how it is when you're in the neighbourhood and get a craving for something sweet."

"I bet. So will it be your usual?" she asked with a little notebook in hand, her eyes dancing with mischief as she subtly looked me over. I must have been quite a sight, dishevelled, mud-splattered, and soaked to the skin.

"Yes please, but just a coke."

She noted that down on the pad. "In a glass?"

"I'd better, or else it dribbles through your fingers."

She laughed at that. "I meant, would you prefer it in a glass or the bottle?"

"Well, as long as it's served by your fair hands, Deb, I'd drink it from Muhammad Ali's old tapdancing shoes."

"Aww… I swear you could turn a girl's head."

I smiled as she did an about-turn and sauntered over to the window to the kitchen with an inviting sway of her hips. It was a very good show.

She'd been working at the Whale since her ex-husband hightailed it out-of-town one morning when he was supposed to be going to work and never looked back, leaving her to fend for their two kids. She talked about them sometimes when it was quiet, and would often entertain me with some of little Timmy and Jackie's adventures.

I enjoyed hearing her talk about her kids, how happy they all were, how normal her life was. It reminded me of those days long ago. When I was no older than little Timmy and Jackie and the world seemed just like a big game. Her stories made me wonder about what might have been before my world got ripped apart...

"There you are," Debra announced cheerfully, laying a tray loaded with food down on the table

I made an appreciative hum as I took in the meal. A big fat bacon double cheeseburger with all the trimmings and a side of chips. The Beached Whale would not win any Michelin stars any time soon, but the fry cook knew what the customers wanted and delivered it.

And a good burger is one thing a kid growing up on the mean streets of New York learns to appreciate, quick.

Say what you like about dive bars. They made the best burgers. Give them a side of Aberdeen Angus, two baps, some cheese and onions, and a few king

Edwards, and they'll serve you up a gastronomic orgy, for the good old price of $4.99. Eat your heart out Ronald McDonald.

"Will there be anything else, sugar pie?" she asked, laying the glass of coke and ice on the table beside the plate.

I sighed and gave her a regretful smile. "Not now, love, we're both on the clock."

"Aww… well, a girl can dream, can't she?" She pouted at me before turning on her heel and sashaying back over to the bar to watch the game with Mike. No sooner had she turned away however than I started on my burger, biting into it with relish.

Holding it in my left hand, I used my right to fish my phone out of my pocket, along with Mr Ritter's list. As I took my next bite, I started researching the next name on the list, but there wasn't much to find. Just his shop's website and social media pages, a few details about his college lectures. Nothing very informative, though his name was mentioned in reference to a civil war that had been going on in Africa. I made a mental note to double check that later.

I was just stashing the phone away in my pocket when the pub door opened, letting in a gust of cool autumn air fragrant with ocean salt. Quick footsteps hurried across the wooden floor to the bar, causing Mike to turn away from the screen. "You're late."

"Sorry!" the newcomer apologised hurriedly, shrugging off her raincoat and stowing it over the bar. "I'm so sorry, it won't happen again."

"That's what you said last time, and yet here you are, late again. What's the matter? Can't you tell time? Your shift started half an hour ago and I-"

"Oh, leave her alone, *Marcus*. When was the last time you ever arrived on time?" Debra admonished. Surprised by her interruption, the bartender only gaped, looking as if he was struggling for what to say, before he just gave up and turned back to the tv, his mouth moving silently as he grumbled under his breath. Satisfied, Debra nodded before putting a hand on the other woman's shoulder. "You ok lovey?"

"Yeah, sorry, I didn't mean to be late. It's just my dad's back is playing him up again, and he needed my help around the store, and time just got away from me."

"Ahh well, *ain't* you just a sweety. Don't worry about it, sugar. Take it from me. So long as you make up your time at the end of your shift, no one will say a thing. We all got our own troubles, you know." Debra shot Mike a look. "Ain't that right, *Marcus*..."

Still chastened, the bartender just grunted in acknowledgement.

"See. Don't worry about it."

The other woman nodded. "Thanks."

Debra was all smiles once more. "Don't mention it. I've still got twenty minutes till the end of my shift. Why don't you go get freshened up? I'll man the fort," she promised, turning away before a sudden thought struck her and nodded in the direction of the pool table. "Oh, watch yourself. The boys back there have been doing nothing but shooting pool and knocking back pints, so they'll be getting pretty rowdy soon."

I tried to focus on my meal but couldn't help eavesdropping and found my eyes drawn to her as she passed my booth. She was young, scarcely into her twenties, barely more than a slip of a girl, but beautiful. A luscious dusky beauty with a firm mouth, strong cheekbones and thick dark mane of hair that tumbled down to the small of her back. She'd dressed smart but casually, in a simple black button up top that only hinted at athletic build and bosom, but alongside slender blue jeans that went down mile upon mile of long legs but always drew the eyes back up to the swells of her derriere.

Captivated by subtle movements of what must have been the most magnificent ass I had ever seen, my eyes remained riveted until she had slipped through the door to the game room. There was a shout of applause from within, and I had no choice but to return my attention to my burger. Yet I could only brood over the feast, my hunger diminished in favour of more carnal appetites as my head swam with thoughts of her walking by. I was going to have to make a point of finding out her name before I-

There was a raucous of laughter and a raspy voice slurred something as the girl came almost running out of the gaming room, head down and tying an apron around her waist. Behind her, a pair of tattoo sleeved arms threw the swinging doors back open before they could completely close in her wake. By my best guess, the man that followed was around my age, between late twenties and early to mid thirties, with a broad, powerful build that his tee and jeans were just tight enough to show off. Beneath his short-cropped hair, his forehead was shiny with perspiration and his squashed face was a flushed ruby colour. His eyes were glassy as he pursued the girl to the bar, yet he carried himself without sway or stumble.

Debra's assessment had been quite accurate in all but one aspect. He wasn't just well on his way to getting rowdy; he was on the road to an awesome bender, and he'd just found his next amusement of the afternoon.

He practically draped himself across the bar as she went behind it to don an apron branded with a carton whale stranded on a beach. "Come have a drink with us."

"I'm sorry, I can't. I'm already running late," she said politely but with her back to him, trying to knot her apron's ties.

"Aw come on now, don't be like that," he cooed, like she was a sulky child in need of placating.

At his back, his companions were filing out of the games room. There were four of them, all with the same ruby checks, and dark glints in their eyes, and as they joined him at the bar, I remembered an old animal documentary I'd watched once about a troop of baboons that had set upon and devoured a baby antelope. These boys had the same look, the same swagger, the same dark energy of beasts on the hunt, looking for trouble.

"Yeah, nobody's gonna say nothin'," one of them sneered, reaching out to stroke her arm. He was a broad-shouldered man with a heavily lined face and a thick salt and pepper goatee beard. She deftly sidestepped, but another one was already waiting to catch her, his fingers just brushing across her derriere as she passed. He leered at her smugly as she backed away, but there was nowhere to go. They had backed her up against the bar. Playing dumb to her distress, Mike kept his face riveted to the screen.

The little twat.

"See, nobody's gonna care," Tattoo Sleeves pressed again. "Come on, have a drink with us. Just a small one. You know you want to."

"No, please, I've got work to do," she refused again, still polite, but with a note to her voice now as she looked for some sort of escape.

Noticing my now half-empty glass, I gulped down the last of the soft drink then held it up high in the drunkard's age-old call for a refill.

She saw my signal and nodded, but her distraction caused one baboon to look my way. It was the one that had touched her backside. A suety faced middle-aged guy that had tried to disguise his balding pate with a greasy top knot. Upon seeing me, his leer fell away to an almost accusing glare. He nudged the man beside him, who, in turn, looked, gawked, then nudged the man beside him. Soon, all five were glowering at me. It was like an absurd game of Monkey see, Monkey do. They obviously hadn't realised they were no longer the only customers.

"Yeah, what do you want?" Topknot asked mockingly.

"A drink." I just smiled back at them and shook my glass again. "Same again, love."

"Coming right up, Sir," the girl called, pouring me another glass of coke from the tap. However, no sooner had she stepped out and around the bar hatch, then she found her way blocked.

"Nah, never mind him, *love*," Tattoo sleeves mocked, emitting my accent to ridiculous levels as he took the glass from her, knocked back a mouthful before spitting it back into the glass, then put it down on the nearest table. He looked back at me, grinned again as he wiped his mouth with the back of his hand. "All yours."

That made them guffaw.

Gritting my teeth, I forced myself to grin right back at him. "Thank you, waiter."

The smirk dropped, but perhaps having already decided he'd got a better hit in, Tattoo turned back to the girl. Removed from what little protection the bar had offered, she suddenly found herself surrounded as they boxed her in, like dogs hunting a doe.

"*Now come on, love.*" Top Knot sang, with an attempt at my accent that would have made even Keanu Reeves wince.

"Yeah, why are you being like this?" asked a heavier man with a pock-marked face, wearing a red trucker's t-shirt under a leather jacket.

"You're safe with us," promised the third of the group, a thinner, hawk-faced man with bleached blonde hair and dressed in jeans and a faded brown leather jacket.

Salt and Pepper reached out to draw slow, intricate patterns up and down her arm. "All we want is one little drink."

"See?" Tattoo Sleeves barked, stepping closer, as good as pinning her against the bar. "Come on, be nice for a change and have a drink with us. You never know. You might like-"

"I said no!" she snapped, her voice hot with anger as she shoved him back, her small hands slamming against his barrel chest as she tried to force her way through. "Just leave me alone will you, alright? I don't want to have a drink with you. I just want to do my job-Ah!"

Her words fell away in a gasp of pain as a big, tattooed paw collared one of her wrists and wrenched her around.

"You bitch!" the man growled, wrenching both her arms behind her back. Her face twisted with pain as he forced her hands at such an angle it forced her back ramrod straight. "Who do you think you are? Don't you know who I am? I'm sick of your stuck up attitude, you little Eskimo whore." He was bending down to speak into her ear, but he was so drunk on anger and booze, his voice carried all around the room. My hands fisted on the tabletop. "You should be grateful they even let your kind in here, rather than keep all you Indian animals chained up on that piece of shit reservation."

"Roy! That is enough!" Debra barked out, storming over to them. "Let her go now!"

She had been staying out of the fray, not approving, but knowing she had to let the new girl figure it out for herself. Such things were part of the job, after all. Desperate or not, if she couldn't handle the odd few handy punters, this clearly wasn't the job for her, but this had gone too far.

"Shut your mouth, Debbi, you're just jealous we're not after that loose cunt of your-"

Tattoo Sleeves, or rather Roy, was so distracted by his own rambling, he didn't hear me get up from my booth. Neither did any of his cackling troop of baboons see me approaching until I'd picked up the glass of coke he'd backwashed.

The dark, frothy contents hit him square in the face, effectively putting a stop to the shit spewing out of his mouth.

The silence seemed to drag on as all the eyes in the room turned on me.

Holding Roy's wild gaze, I put the glass back on the table where he'd left it. "I'm sick of hearing you talk."

"You know what I am?" he snarled in a voice that was suddenly distinctively Russian. Pissed off Russian, if there was any other kind.

"Drunk. Stupid. Ugly all day," I offered, even as I felt my insides knot and writhe like snakes. Of all the bloody bully boy pissheads in this whole goddamn state, why did it have to be Russians?

"I'm the guy that's gonna rip your fucking face off." The mix of his north-west American accent spoken in the Russian voice made him sound like a mafia bad guy in a politically incorrect 80s action movie. His fluent command of English grammar, however, suggested he was a born and bred all American, rather than the thousands of Russian-born immigrants that came into the states every year.

Of Washington state's near eight million population, nearly five hundred thousand were descendants of Mother Russia.

In hindsight, that might have made my choice to hide out there rather questionable, given my less than stellar history with the Russian Mafia, but then it wasn't something they were likely to plaster all over their 'Evergreen State' postcards, was it. They needed to keep a few surprises for the guidebooks.

"Oh?" I forced a pleasant smile. "Well, till then, the lady said no. So it's time to go."

"She'll be saying a lot more by the time I'm done with her," he sneered and looked down at the girl, whose arms he still pinned behind her back. She just stared at me with wide, terrified eyes. She didn't even seem to notice that the coke rivulets had now started running off Roy's face into her thick curtain of dark hair.

"Maybe, but not today." I dropped the act. Time to get serious. "No means no. She's not interested. So shut up and fuck off, because if I have to listen to any more filth come spewing out your cunt mouth, the next thing out of it will be your teeth."

"Yeah? I'd like to see you tr-"

His taunt died in a loud, wet smack as my fist smashed into his jaw. It wasn't my best, but it got the job done. Caught by surprise, he reeled backward, releasing the girl to clamp his hands over his mouth. The girl turned and ran between two of the encircling bodies and Debra pulled her close, out of the line of fire.

The troop just looked amongst themselves, unsure what to do next.

When Roy's hands came away, they were a wet and sticky red. He spat a mouthful of blood to the floor, and a rather yellow tooth bounced under a table, out of sight. He glared at me in unchecked fury, his face going as red as the blood dribbling out of his chops. "Motherfucker, you knocked out my fucking tooth!"

"Well, I warned you, now why don't you sleep it off before you taste some real pain."

"Taste this!" Red-faced and almost blind with rage, Roy came at me like a bull, his bloodied fist swinging in a wide arc to take my head off my shoulders. I didn't wait for it to fall, just stepped in close and jabbed mine straight into his solar plexus. He gasped as the hit made contact, made all the more incapacitating by the momentum of his mad rush. He'd be feeling it for weeks, and as he folded over in pain, I stepped back, grabbed his grey top, and brought his head down onto the edge of the nearest table.

Somewhere, people were shouting, screaming for someone to stop. Other things were said, but that was all I caught. I wasn't listening. They were only distractions now, and I couldn't afford to get distracted. Sidestepping Roy's body as it slumped to the floor, I back stepped, grabbed up the coke glass from the table where I'd left it and brought it round into the side of Trucker top's face as he came at me. It exploded on contact, leaving my hand stinging and him with a few more scars to add to his collection.

Hawk Face was right behind him. Literally, he let Trucker take the hit so that, as the bigger man went down, he could pounce. His right fist cracked against my temple, a jarring blow that made stars dance across my eyes for a second before his left hand grabbed my shoulder to drag me back for another. Bad move. On pure reflex, my knee came up to meet his groin. Then, as my right swung up to meet the inside of his left elbow, breaking his hold and throwing him off balance, I stepped back to bring him further forward before bringing my left elbow up to meet his oncoming nose. The crack of shattering cartilage was almost deafening that close and the blood that fountained out of his broken nose would have nearly painted my face if I hadn't followed up with a hard kick that sent him tumbling backward over a table.

Then I was backtracking as Trucker came at me, one side of his face red from brow to chin. Not that I was scared. I just had to keep moving. That was how to win a fight when outnumbered. It didn't matter how big and strong you were. Stay in one spot for too long and the bad guys would converge on you and beat you down. If you kept moving and hit hard and fast, you could take them down one by one.

Only it seemed Salt and Pepper knew that rule too, because as I twisted around a table I glimpsed him circling round to meet me, and behind him, Top Knot had blocked the way through to the games room. It was a smart move, but they'd also cocked up.

Almost halfway between me and Salt and Pepper, there was a serving tray on a table. Debra had put it there when she went to help the new girl. It was little more than a sheet of cheap plastic, like the ones in McDonald's or Burger King, but it would do the job.

Throwing a blind hand out as I continued back stepping, grabbed the plastic and swung it up and around in a high arc that met the bloody side of Trucker's face. I doubt it would have added to the shit storm of pain the glass exploding against his face had dealt him, but the hit was enough to knock him down across a table. My body pivoted with the swing, twisting to confront Salt and Pepper as he ran around the next table to block me off and, having drawn my arm back, I jabbed the edge of the tray into the apple of his throat. He dropped like a sack of old potatoes, his hands clawing at his neck, but all that came out of his mouth was a gurgle.

I didn't think about Top Knot, didn't plan what to do about him. I just know he was not about to come to me. He was playing it smart, making me come to him. So I did, in a manner. Instead of just running at him, a flick of my wrist sent the tray spinning out of my hand, across the room and into his abdomen. He doubled over with the hit, groaning. Even so, he still tried to swing for me. It was a decent effort, but winded, he lacked the balance to carry it through. I blocked it, slamming the meat of my left hand into his hooked elbow, holding it there mid-swing as my right smashed into his balls. He screamed at that. I couldn't blame him for that. The only thing worse than a hit to the bollocks was a kneecapping. That didn't mean I was about to take it easy on him though and with his knees suddenly turned to jelly, all it took was a pivot to throw him through the swinging doors and across the pool table.

Except, then something hard shattered against my shoulder and I stumbled right in there after Top Knot, the table edge-rushing up to give my ribs some good news.

I just got my hands up in time to brace, but the hit was like taking a swing from a baseball bat. Biting back on the roar of pain as my front seemed to combust beneath my shirt and jacket, I threw a glance back. Trucker Top was back for more and followed me through the doors and brandished the bottle he'd just broken on my back like a knife. Behind him, Salt and Pepper, and Hawk Face, were pulling themselves together, and I could hear Top Knot's feet dancing a jig as he tried to climb back up.

Things were about to get messy.

Then I spotted an old glass ashtray sitting on the side of the table and drove my leg backwards in a kick that Trucker must have walked right into because I felt the heel of my boot meet soft meat. He let out a strangled noise, but I had already pulled my leg back and was twisting away before he could slash at me with the bottle. In one move, I'd scooped up the ashtray and pivoted round to face him as he stumbled back a step. Then I was going at him, forcing the bottle aside with one hand, punching the ashtray into the core of his throat with the other, driving him back against the closest wall before kicking his knee out from under him. He went down hard, choking and spluttering as his hands grasped at his throat like he was trying to undo an invisible necktie that had been pulled too tight.

Something clanked to my left, and I glimpsed Top Knot pulling a Pool Cue from the rack on the wall. Wish I'd seen that. One of those would have made this a walk in the park.

Judging by that big stupid grin on his face, Top Knot thought so too. Though judging by the way he held it, that was his only idea. He certainly didn't have the foggiest how to handle it. He just swung it up above his head and ran at me, screaming like the dumb hillbilly bad guy in a Steven Seagal film. Fortunately, old Steve always knew just how to handle them.

I wasn't quite a Zen master, but when the bad guy came running at you and you were holding a weight of solid glass, it didn't matter. Cranking back my arm, I hurled the ashtray at him.

There was no time to aim, but he was so close, I didn't need to.

It rebounded off his jaw with a sickening thud and skidded under the table, sending his swing way off course as I stepped in with a brain-rattling hook that I retracted and turned into an elbow jab. He fell back a step, but then recovered enough to come at me with the cue again, swinging it in a wide hay scything arc. It missed by miles and cut over the table with a high whistle, dragging him around, exposing his back. It was too good of an opportunity to miss. Grabbing that stupid fucking Top Knot, I gave it a hard jerk that dragged his head back and down, so his own weight threw him across the table and knocked the fight right out of him.

That left only Salt and Pepper, and Hawk Face to go. They'd pulled themselves together and were half running, half stumbling through the mess of tables and chairs. Dragging the cue from Top Knot's limp fingers, I turned to meet them.

Hawk Face came first this time and was greeted by a quick sweep of the cue's point that smacked him across the head and sent him skidding right. I followed, pivoting and stabbing the cue's butt back into Salt and Pepper's midriff as he came through the doors. He doubled over, and I left the stick there just long enough to brace my kick into Hawk's balls. Then I twisted back around to face Salt, retracting the cue and then reversing it in my hands so the butt swung up to crack against his jaw before a round kick sent him through the swing doors as I brought the cue around in a swing across Hawk's ribs. He bent with it, his mouth opening in a scream that died away as my knee came up to meet him with a wet smack.

He crumpled to the floor, curling into a ball, not out cold but definitely feeling very sorry for himself. A quick glance around confirmed the others wouldn't be feeling up to another round anytime soon. Dumping the cue onto the table, I turned my back on the carnage, pushed back through the swinging doors, and came face to face with Roy.

He looked like a mess. A bloody mess. A right bloody mess. Head wounds had a habit of bleeding a lot and the meeting between his head and the table had opened up a gash across his temple that was leaking down his face. But it was the knife in his hand that caught my attention. An NR-40, the soviet fighting knife that was issued throughout the Red Army after the Winter War revealed the Soviet force lacked a good close-quarters weapon and had seen service throughout the Second World War. It had long since been taken out of the official military kit, but, rather than vanish from history; it had become one of the favourite toys of Russian Organised Crime. A deadly weapon that comprised a smooth wooden grip painted black, an S-guard, and a single-edged 152mm blade that was stabbing straight for my chest.

In any other moment, that would have been me done. Fast reflexes were good, but they could only carry a body so far. In the end, everything always came down to limitations, and I was at mine. Roy was too close, and while he certainly wasn't faster than me, he had the element of surprise, but I had luck. I always had a certain sort of luck. The sort of twisted luck that meant you got caught in traffic and missed your non-refundable flight, only to learn later that same flight crashed into the Rocky Mountains.

I was lucky because at any other moment this guy might have waited before trying to knife me, taking the time to gather his wits or regroup his senses. As it was, he was dizzy from the knock to the head, and losing all that blood now smeared across his face had to be having an effect because he missed that last vital step to stab the knife home. He overextended himself and I grabbed his knife hand and pulled it even further off course as I stepped outside the blade, then into him. Swinging a left hook that cracked against his cheekbone, I then dropped the arm down, wrapping it around his extended arm before pressing down on his wrist with the other.

It was a simple hold, but one that gave the user absolute control of the subject with minimum use of force.

I didn't press down hard, just enough for him to get the message.

Either drop the blade, or I'd break his arm.

He tried to fight my grip. Tried to flex and tense and bend the limb the right way, gritting the teeth he had left and glaring daggers at me even as his back arched up to ease the agony searing up the length of his arm. So I pressed down with a little more insistence. He got the message. His fingers opened immediately with a small gasp of pain and I scooped the NR-40 up mid-fall. No sooner had I released his arm than my knee was driving up into his, making his legs buckle and I urged him down to the tiled floor.

"You shouldn't play with knives," I mocked, grabbing and twisting Roy's arms behind his back, pinning them there with my knee.

"Fuck you, Limey piece-a shit," he spluttered, no doubt his ego refusing to admit defeat without the show of defiance.

"Now, what did I tell you about that mouth of yours?" Noticing the knife's case strapped to the back of his belt, I quickly unhooked it, sheathed the steel, then pocketed it. A man always had need of a good knife.

"Fuck you, shithead," he cursed again, spitting out a mouthful of blood and spittle in his rage. His eyes burned with fury as he tried twisting round to look at me. "You best enjoy this moment, because when *we* get through with you, you'll be begging for death. We'll kill your friends, your family, everyone you ever loved. Enjoy this moment, bitch, because we're about to bring your world burning down around you."

Too late, someone else already did.

"Alright, that's enough out of you," I barked angrily, tired of the sound of his voice. It sorely tempted me to knock him out when a small gasp reached my ears from the other side of the dining room. My eyes darted up to see Debra, Max, and the girl clustered behind the bar. But it was the girl who caught my eyes, the look of horror on her face.

It gave me a better idea.

Lifting my foot from the small of Roy's back, I grabbed his wrists and heaved him up to his feet. He struggled and twisted as if to break free, but the effort lacked strength and was probably more for himself than anything. Either way, it didn't impede me from dragging him over to the bar. "Now be a good boy and apologise to the ladies?"

The three onlookers just stared at me in absolute horror, like I was a raving lunatic, but I didn't care. This bastard couldn't do anything to me. No one in the Whale knew me. No one knew my name or where I lived. I always paid in cash, came on odd days and didn't even use the Wi-Fi. His threat was all talk, but it brought back the memories, memories that got me worked, memories of fire and blood, of his mother's screams, of watching his dad's getting blown away, of the New York City back streets, of watching men he'd known for years turning on him. And all at the hands of the Russian Mafia.

This bastard may not have had any hand in that, but he was part of the organisation. and thought that meant he could scare me. He and his troop of baboons thought they were hard men, but they were just bullies that got off on tormenting people smaller and weaker than them. And I'd show him for the cowards they were, even if it was only for my sick amusement and warped sense of right and wrong.

I might have been a bastard, but I had standards, and I didn't like men that hit girls.

He twisted his head around and sneered.

"Fuck you bitc-ahh!" he gasped, throwing his head back in pain as I swung my elbow up into the part of his back over his right kidney. His body bucked underneath me as the spasm and pain-wracked him and I had to resist the urge to smile grimly as even before I asked again, he was jabbering, "I'm sorry, I'm sorry…"

I let him go, and he dropped to the floor and writhed like a worm in bleach. It was a disappointing end. I'd been hoping he could take the pain a little longer, but it was too late now. His kidneys would've given him hell for a while, so if anyone asked, I could always say the kick I then gave his face was mercy.

Actually, I just didn't want to hear his blubbering.

Then I turned my gaze back to the three behind the bar, my attention focusing on the girl, still wearing that same frightened look. I did my best to smile comfortingly. "You alright love?"

She reeled back at the question like a viper had suddenly reared up before her. She just stared at me with that same look of undisguised terror. "Don't… please… just, just go."

Then she turned and ran around the bar and bolted past me in a flight back through the game room to the back rooms. And as she vanished from sight, the fry cook pushed through the swinging game room doors to survey the carnage, a big man in a white apron, holding one of the biggest knives I'd ever seen, and I decided that going probably wasn't a bad idea.

"Sorry about the mess," I said while fishing a few fifty-dollar bills out of my wallet and putting them on the bar, before I turned and walked back outside.

The cloud canopy was gone, turning it into a beautiful autumn afternoon. Typical.

I was just about to climb back into the 911, but I couldn't resist a final look back at the Beached Whale and thought of the girl with dark hair and a cute bum, and wondered what might have been, if only she'd been on time.

Guess I'll never know her name now…

Chapter Three

The second name on my list took me just down the road to Port Angeles.

With a population of about twenty thousand within an area of fourteen square miles, more than a quarter of which extended out into the Salish sea, Port Angeles wasn't exactly a large city.

Built upon the deep natural harbour, the Spanish explorer Francisco de Eliza had named it Puerto de Nuestra Señora de los Ángeles in 1791. Francisco

landed there on his return trip to the Spanish base at
Nootka Sound after a failed expedition of the Georgia
Strait and had immediately claimed the land for Spain
despite it already being well populated by the
indigenous people. From then on until the mid-
nineteenth century, it was largely a trading port
between the native tribes and Europeans travelling
through the area. Ship by ship, caravan by caravan,
the travellers settled the area and transformed it into
a shipping and whaling town. Developers followed,
and before the turn of the century, its population had
bloomed from three hundred to over three thousand.
The USA incorporated it in 1890 and over the next
century, its focus had switched from fishing, to
logging, and now to tourism.

Professor David Riley hadn't adapted to the latest
change too well.

He owned a fishing and game sporting goods store
just off the 101. A convenient location for business,
but one that came with steep rates in the current
economy. Also, in a society where public opinion was
switching from trophy hunting to conservation,
shooting was no longer good business.

He was also a part-time professor of archaeology
at the University of Washington. A minor role in the
faculty that required him to hold a minimum of three
lectures a week, but one that allowed him to pursue
his lifelong passion for the past. A passion that, like

so many others, he had allowed to spiral out of control and lead him down a road of endless trouble.

His adventures had unfortunately led him to Ritter's door and Ritter to mine. With my arrival, the circle was complete, and the journey written, although the destination remained to be seen. Compared to earlier, this should be a walk in the park.

Riley wasn't like Jasper. He didn't have muscle to call in and put the frighteners on whatever poor bugger came to collect their due. He was a professor, a learned man, a talker. He'd try to talk his way out, appeal to my sense of reason or compassion, but he wouldn't fight. Maybe he'd try to run, but I rather doubted that.

He was the sort that wanted to pay his due.

The sort that just needed a little help to adjust their priorities.

And that's where I came in.

Google said that Riley's store, Wild Frontier, was open until seven in the evening.

By the time I pulled into the car park of the storage warehouse next door, the clock on the 911's dash showed that it was a little past two thirty. So, I just shut the engine down, reclined my seat back to stretch my legs out, and waited.

It always helped to know a bit about the target before confronting them, and a little observation could tell you an awful lot about a target's situation.

Debt collection wasn't all twisting arms and breaking windows until the deadbeat coughed up with the cash they were hiding under their mum's mattress. Only thugs treated it as a carte blanche to deal out beatings, and they were rarely in the business long. It was essential to have a brain for this sort of work, not just muscle. You had to get the measure of your mark, had to be good at reading people and judging how far you could push them. You also had to know which just needed a slap and which required motivation.

As a rule of thumb, everyone who borrowed money had what they owed in their possession when the time came to pay it back, in one form or another. A warehouse full of last season's stock. An expensive luxury watch hidden in the sock draw. The diamond earrings the mistress didn't wear anymore. Even the car just sitting there in the drive when there was a bus stop just down the street.

They had the money. My job was to make them see it, and then get their priorities in order.

After all, what was more important? Pawning their parents' wedding rings and paying off their debts, or keeping the gold hidden away in the mattress and losing the use of their knees. They didn't always like my solutions, but most saw sense and their debts got sorted.

Yet, as I watched the slow trickle of pedestrians walking by the Wild Frontier's big window displays, my mind kept wandering back to the events at the Whale in Distress.

That look on the girl's face when I asked if she was alright.

Had I terrified her that much?

I hadn't held back, sure. Those baboons sure weren't pulling their punches, so why should I? But the violence hadn't been worse than anything she'd have seen before.

Then again, why did it even bother me? It wasn't as if I'd ever see her again. I didn't even know her name. What did it matter what she thought of me?

All the same, it bothered me. It shouldn't have, but it did.

I'd tried to help her, but she ran away and left me looking like a right arsehole.

I didn't know whether I should go back and apologise, or be pissed on general principle.

Oh fuck it, it wasn't my problem anymore. I needed to quit thinking about her. Distraction was the number one cause of all fuckups in my line of work, and if I fucked up, it would turn into a real bad day, real quick. I was working. I needed to be professional and keep my mind on the job.

So I did, but time can have a habit of dragging its feet whenever you're waiting. My disobedient brain jumped back to the scene about a dozen times before the alarm on my phone started going off, warning me it was a quarter to seven. I hadn't needed it. In my restlessness, I'd checked the car clock every five minutes or so, but it never hurt to have a backup.

Silencing it with a swipe of my thumb, I climbed out, grabbed my jacket from the parcel shelf where it had been drying in the sun, and pulled it on. The 911 locked with a click of the fob and I crossed the semi-deserted convenience store car park to Wild Frontier's porch. The store logo, an oval depicting the outline of mountains behind the shaggy silhouette of a brown bear, was stamped on both of the sliding doors and embossed on the enormous sign that stretched across the top of the storefront.

Someone obviously believed it paid to advertise.

Inside, it was everywhere. On pens and keychain, fridge magnets and drink glasses and travel bottles, all hanging and arranged around the checkout tills. They even had it plastered on tents and sleeping bags, all of which sat in one corner set up to look like a small campsite scene straight out of Jellystone Park. All that was missing was Ranger Smith chasing a picnic basket snatching Yogi Bear.

Maybe Yogi and Boo-Boo had taken shelter in the clothing department. There certainly were plenty of hiding places amidst the waterproofs, camo overalls, shirts and trousers, boots, socks, gloves, beanies and just about anything the typical Rambler could want. And it had all got the logo treatment. There were other brands, too, but it was lower of the range stuff, the cheap and cheerful brands- not much from North Face.

And then there were the guns. Rows of them sat heavily along the back wall. Rifles and shotguns of every kind and calibre- enough of them to fight a small war- were all safely secured behind the security glass. Professor David Reilly was working there, manhandling three big boxes branded with logos I didn't recognise.

The professor didn't exactly have the Indiana Jones vibe, but he made a half decent impression, even missing the fedora and whip. He was wiry and lean in his Wild Frontier's branded check shirt and jeans, with a shiny bald crown encircled by a collar of white brush and a thick snowy lord Kitchener moustache that drooped down past the chin of his long face.

Courtesy of the lack of a bell on the door, he was blissfully unaware he had a new customer, so I went over to examine the weapons. I didn't need him to notice me yet. In fact, it would serve my needs better if he didn't.

I did a quiet perusal of the rifles, paying particular attention to the models and the rather high price tags. Someone must have been trying to rebuild their bank balance, double quick. Either that, or they were pretty desperate.

And it wasn't just the big guns that were overpriced. There were pistols and revolvers, too. Those ranged from big hunting revolvers to the tiny shooters ladies kept in their handbags and that made their attackers appreciate their remaining ball. The weapons were all solemnly arranged in display cases, along with all the usual collections of accessories and boxes of ammo.

There was even a selection of bows and, much to my amusement, a few crossbows.

Seeing a few out on display, I couldn't resist picking up one of the bigger models and giving it a once over. The label said it was a *Thunderbolt X10*, and had the legend *'The only thing faster is light'* scrolled along the butt in the style of a lightning bolt. There also was a cartoon sketch of a hunter dressed up like Elmer Fudd firing it at an advancing grizzly.

"That's quite a rig. You like it?"

I glanced up and saw the good Professor Riley walking up to me, giving his best big and friendly grin between his mustachios.

"Yeah, it feels a bit light for me though," I told him, making a show of weighing it with my hands before putting it back down on the display. "And personally, I prefer something with a bit more stopping power. Bit more bang, you know what I mean? You wouldn't happen to have an M&P 10 out the back, would you?"

"Oh, you a fan of Smith & Wesson?" he asked in a pleasant, softly spoken voice rich with the exaggerated punctuation that only came from a good Oxford or Cambridge education. Much more David Attenborough than Indiana Jones, but tempered by a north-western drawl. That didn't stop him beaming with a look that might as well have turned his eyes to dollar signs. In his position, I guess that was a fair one. Since the 70s, when big bold Harry Callahan had walked onto the silver screen with his 44, Smith & Wesson had become the gun of choice for all True Blue Americans. This meant they were also expensive, and if the prices I'd seen already were anything to go by, this place would charge a literal arm and leg.

"Who isn't? Clint Eastwood's 'do you feel lucky?' Blow your head clean off and all that crap," I lied, forcing myself to grin like just another wannabe gunslinger.

Not that S&W were a bad choice. They had produced some excellent gear. I'd just never gotten attached to any particular weapon. So long as you can hit your target, pretty much any gun would do the job. The rest was just semantics for gunsmiths and salespeople.

"Right," he said, still beaming, not missing a trick as he walked up to the display case and gestured his hand out. "Well… no, I'm afraid we're all out. But there is a very nice Remington 783 over here that you might like to have a look at."

I ignored his suggestion. Clicking my tongue thoughtfully, I made a show of perusing the wall of rifles. "Oh, that's a shame. Well, what about a Bushmaster AR-15 Predator?"

"Err… No, sorry." His smile dropped slightly for a moment. The AR was about as controversial a weapon in the States as it was possible to get after it had become the weapon of choice for the perpetrators of mass shootings. However, that hadn't stopped the NRA from dubbing it *America's rifle*.

Selling guns but not having at least one AR-15 in stock was akin to having a gun control sticker on the till.

Desperate then, good.

"Waiting on delivery?" I asked, smiling pleasantly.

"Something like that…" He nodded, the wheels in his head turning. "If you don't mind me saying, mister, you don't look much like a hunter."

Oh, how did you do it, Holmes? Between my leather jacket, oxford shirt, faded Levis and Doc

Martens, I looked about as much a Davy Crockett wannabe as he did a Freddy Mercury tribute act.

"Well, that's probably because I've never been game hunting in my life," I chuckled dryly. "But a man always needs a good gun to uphold his constitutional rights."

He relaxed a little at that. "You mean household security?"

"Something like that," I parroted, to let his mind jump to its own conclusions.

Beaming again, he waved a hand at the wall of weapons. "Well, everything I have here will more than keep your house safe at night. Though I'll need to see a weapons licence and go through the standard checks the state requires for-"

"Ah yes, about that," I cut in. "A mutual friend of ours suggested you might have a way of getting around all the red tape, *Professor Riley*."

"Excuse me?"

Perhaps it was the implied familiarity, or just my use of his previously unmentioned name, but Professor Riley suddenly had a look on his face like he was sucking a lemon under that moustache.

"Mr Ritter," I offered, still smiling.

And just like that, he went as white as his Lord Kitchener. "What do you want?"

"Now, no need to be like that. I'm just here to talk," I put in quickly, hands raised with palms out in my best non-threatening pose.

"I… see," he nodded, yet even as he said it, his eyes were side-lining towards the wall of rifles. His lips quivered nervously. "I was just about to lock up for the night, so maybe we should take this somewhere more private."

Dropping my hand, I feigned ignorance of the idea forming in his head.

"What a good idea. You go lock up. Don't want anyone sneaking in and stealing anything now, do you?" At my agreeing to his plan, his face all but lit up, so it was with no small amount of amusement I added, "I'll just wait here."

He nodded and quickly did an about turn, fishing out a big ring of keys from his pocket that jingled merrily as he went to the door. He didn't strike me as the type to throw down, but if he was as desperate as I thought, I had better not take the chance of leaving him alone with all this firepower. Desperate men were capable of desperate acts. Which was also why I kept a close eye on him as he thrust a key into the lock. I didn't blink until I was certain he'd locked it and was on his way back.

He'd of had to be the worst kind of fool to run now, but the line between desperate and foolhardy could be perilously fine at times.

When he came scurrying back, his moustache still quivering, I half expected him to start flapping. Instead, he just came up to me and stood stoic, waiting for my next instruction. I motioned for him to lead on. "After you."

"Oh…" He looked surprised and then realised I would obviously not know the way. "Of-of course, err… this way."

He led me down the wall of rifles to a backdoor nestled between boxes of arrow shafts and a stack of discounted camping gear, through into what must have been a combination of storage space and a loading bay. Huge loading doors made up most of the left side wall. They had converted the rest of the space into aisles, three shelves high and just wide enough in between each for a set of aircraft steps. They'd loaded each shelf high and tight, with packing cases of every shape and size.

Just to the right of the door we'd come through, there was a spiralling wrought iron staircase up to an above catwalk and a suspended complex of rooms. I followed Professor Riley up into one that I guessed he'd made into an office. There was a large wooden desk with a computer monitor on top and a big chair behind it along one wall, a matching-style filing cabinet and a bookcase on either side. One corner made up a kitchenette, and another had a small sofa and chair around a coffee table to make up a sitting area.

Professor Riley went straight for the kitchenette. "Coffee?"

I shook my head. "Tea please, milk and two sugars."

He looked up at me, surprised. "English Breakfast or Earl Grey?"

"I'd prefer PG Tips." PG was a popular tea brand in the United Kingdom, but by the look on Riley's face, they'd never made it into his morning brew. "English Breakfast will be fine, thank you."

He nodded and turned back into the kitchen, filling up a small portable kettle from the sink and setting it to the boil. Letting him get on with it, I walked to the desk and gave it a quick once over. The computer was asleep, but there was paperwork scattered across it, bills and invoices, order summaries and what must have been official letters stamped with red. There was no order to it, unless the pieces of pottery and masonry that sat here and there held some significance I'd missed. Chipped and aged, they'd all seen better days, so maybe it was some sort of record of dates. Terracotta for still due, ivory might be first notice, the polished stone for final notice and an implement to break thumbs, maybe.

A photo stood in one corner in a wood frame. It was a family portrait of a man, a woman, and their daughter. The man was obviously Professor Riley, back when his Lord Kitchener was a rich teak and he had a head of hair, sitting straight and poised in his Sunday best. A woman who I guessed was his wife had an arm around him and smiled broadly while a girl, a skinny, gangly little thing just entering her teens, nestled between them with her arms wrapped protectively around a retriever puppy. She had her mother's dark hair and wide smile, but her father's blue eyes and a slightly paler complexion than her mother's bronzed native American heritage.

They looked so happy, happier than any family I'd ever seen. And like I found myself so often doing in these moments, I tried to remember my own parents, and if we'd ever been so happy. Those memories were masked behind a veil of blood and fire, and the sound of my mother's dying screams as she tried to shield me.

"Are you alright?" Professor Riley's voice asked with a hint of concern, jarring me from my reflections. I glanced back to see him placing two steaming mugs down on the coffee table, half watching me with a look that mixed concern and suspicion.

Forcing down the icy, roiling feeling that had frozen my guts, I forced my easy, 'it's all good,' grin into place. "Of course, sorry, I tuned out there for a moment." I was about to join him but then remembered he'd caught me looking at the photo on his desk and added, "You have a beautiful family, Professor Riley."

"Err… thank you." His eyes flickered downward, a dark, almost haunted look flashing across to the surface. A look I knew all too well. It vanished quickly though, when I sunk into the vacant chair. He sat on the opposite end of the sofa and, ignoring his coffee, said. "Please, let me just say how-"

"Well, that's very good of you to offer, Doc, but maybe I better go first," I cut in, knowing what he was about to say, and I was not in the mood to hear it. It was the same every time, the same old lines about best intentions and hard times. It was as if every guy that got caught up in bad debts had watched that scene in Pulp Fiction one too many times and had somehow forgotten how the lines provoked Johnny T and SL Jackson to blow people away.

Just the thought of hearing it again got my fingers twitching to throttle something.

To resist the urge, I wrapped them around the teacup and took a long sip. It wasn't bad, not enough milk, but at least he hadn't made it with a damn microwave.

Putting the cup down, I then steepled my fingers and fixed him with a firm stare.

"Last year, you went to your university board with a proposed expedition to the Congo Rainforest. You'd found evidence of a previously lost city and wanted to hunt for it. Sounds a bit too much like a Michael Crichton novel for my liking, but whatever makes you happy. So, the board rejected your proposal, but rather than accept their decision and call it a day, you attempted to fund the expedition yourself, with little success. After exhausting all other options, you approached our mutual friend, who, after looking over the evidence and being given your professional reassurance that the trip was feasible, wrote you a blank cheque. Hmm… can't say anyone's ever given me one of those. That was some story you must have told him, Doc. Have you ever considered a career in the church?"

"It's all true. The city exists," Professor Riley promised, his voice rising a tad more defensive than I'm sure he meant it to sound.

"If you say so," I shrugged, passing it off. "So, with sufficient funds for your expedition, you chartered a flight to the DRC. You were there a few weeks before returning to Washington on an economy flight. The recent coup d'état in the area had forced you to abandon your expedition, along with all your supplies and equipment."

"It wasn't my fault," Professor Riley protested. "The Government troops seized me at a roadblock, arrested me for espionage and threw me into a cell. They confiscated everything I had, the funds, my passport, even the clothes off my back. There was nothing I could do."

There was a tremor in his voice that made me think he was on the verge of a panic attack, so I raised a hand to calm him.

"I believe you. That's not why I'm here," I said, but couldn't resist adding, "Though, surely you knew the political instability of the region was one of the main reasons the university board had decided your expedition was unfeasible in the first place. I'm guessing you didn't raise that particular point with our mutual friend."

Professor Riley nodded. "No, but I didn't have a choice. I needed his funding," he admitted. "At the time, it looked like the region could break out in civil war at any moment."

"Not a good day to be in Central Africa, then." I took another drink from my tea.

"They could have destroyed the ruins in the fighting if I didn't find them before it all kicked off. It happens all the time. In every war fought, we destroy countless numbers of our historical heritage, and that's when the governments know, or are at least aware, the sites might be there. Imagine how much we've lost, how much we've destroyed and can never get back." His eyes were turning glassy, the very thought alone near enough to bring him to tears. "This site is the only one of its kind. The only mark the tribe ever existed at all. I couldn't let it just get carpet bombed from history."

"Well, I'm not interested in your reasoning, Professor. I'm sure you did what you thought best." I smiled again. It was time to cut through the bullshit. "However, I am interested in how you're planning to repay Mr Ritter, now that your expedition has failed."

His mouth pulled into a tight frown beneath its nest, his lips pressed so tight they turned as pale as his Lord Kitchener, and he seemed genuinely confused. "Well… er, you see, generally speaking, most investors fund university expeditions for charitable reasons and don't expect-"

"Yes," I nodded. "But the University of Washington did not sponsor your expedition. Nor did any other foundation. If they had, I wouldn't be here now, would I?" I took another long draw of my mug. The tea was lukewarm, but I'd had a lot worse in these theatrics and there was a little less than half left when I put it back down. Beside it, Professor Riley's coffee remained untouched. It would be stone cold soon, but maybe that was how he liked it. They say you can't taste cold coffee, after all.

"Mr Ritter isn't a charity organisation or a socialite looking to score points with the local trash mags, Professor. You signed a contract guaranteeing all funds would be repaid, and that you would be fully responsible for the repayment, which stands at seventy-six thousand dollars."

"Oh God," he groaned, the colour seeping from the rest of his face to leave him almost bone white.

I leaned back in the seat. "Yes, I know this must come as a shock. Debts have a habit of building up when not managed properly. That's why our mutual friend has asked me to give you a hand."

It seemed to take an age for my words to sink in, but when they finally did, they hit like a hammer swing. He was still as white as a sheet, but his eyes were set dead on me. Suspicion and defiance burned in their icy blue waters. "What sort of hand?"

Maybe he had a spine in there after all.

"There's no need to look quite so worried, Professor Riley," I offered, holding his gaze. "There's no need for this to be unpleasant. I'm not here to break your legs. Just help you facilitate the repayments."

His frown carved deep lines across his already creased brow. "So you're a debt fixer."

"More like a debt eliminator," I elaborated. "In these trying times, it's common for people to get their priorities confused. I just un-confuse the matter. Now, normally I would propose repossessing an item of equal or greater value than the debt, such as a car, against repayment. But as you drive a Pontiac, I don't really see that working here. You also already mortgaged your house to get the lion's share of the funding for your original expedition, as well as liquidated most of your savings. All this, of course, means your credit is shot to shit, so a loan is out of the question. That just leaves this store."

"You want me to mortgage my store?" The professor jeered, the ends of his moustache quivering with rage.

"Well, that's up to you," I shrugged. This old man was a fool, but I couldn't help liking him. "You've got a lot of nice things here, Professor Riley. Expensive though, perhaps a bit too expensive. A sale might help with that. Or you could sell up, put the stock into storage and go viral. That would cut down on the expenses, don't you think?"

He spluttered, his face suddenly indignant. "But it's not that simple. I can't just sell up at the drop of a hat, and a sale wouldn't work either. If I drop my prices too much, I won't be able to pay my suppliers' fees and then I'll have no stock."

"Switch suppliers," I offered.

"Again, it's not that easy, and then there's the bank to think about. Their interest rates were outrageous. I can't fall back on the repayments to them." He took a breath, trying to get a grip. "Please, understand, I-I can get the money. Tell Mr Ritter he'll get it. I just need a little more time."

Frowning, I sat up. "I see. Well, that's a pity, because Mr Ritter needs his money by Friday."

"What!" Professor Riley lurched to his feet, slamming his hands down onto the tabletop hard enough for coffee to spill over the rim of his untouched mug. "Are you mad? I can't-"

"Sit. Down," I snarled, low and long, and making no effort to blunt the steel in my voice, like I was talking to a kid throwing a paddy and chucking all of his toys out of the pram. It did the trick. Riley slunk back into his seat, though his eyes were trying to burn their protests into my skull.

Right, it was time to introduce the good doctor to the facts of life. "Professor Riley, I appreciate how upsetting this is for you, but you took Mr Ritter's money. Now he wants it back."

He spluttered at that. "Yes, but he never, he never said-"

And what if he had? Would it have made a difference?

"I'm sure he didn't. Or maybe he did, and you didn't hear, or perhaps misunderstood. Who can tell? Be that as it may, he still wants what you owe. The choice is yours."

"Please. I just need more time…" And just like that, the fire left his eyes, and I watched all the energy drain away to show him for what he really was. A tired old man, weak and desperate and grabbing at whatever straw he could see.

"Don't we all. But then again, we rarely get a choice in these things," I spat the words out, barely able to stomach them. A mix of pity and revulsion turning my stomach. "Me, for instance. I'd much rather have another cup of this tea on Friday morning than break your legs. Still, you'll be amazed at how easy things become once properly motivated."

It was time to go. Standing, I forced my pleasant smile back into place. "Thank you for the tea. I'll be back on Friday. Good luck with the sale."

The professor didn't get up. He didn't make any acknowledgment at all. He just sat there, hunched over and broken, so I left him there in his office. The shop front was all locked up, but I'd spotted the back door in the warehouse on the way up, so instead I went that way, smacking the push lever and emerging out into the reversing slipway for delivery vehicles.

I followed the slip road around aimlessly, not really caring where it led, so long as it was away from Wild Frontier.

The whole encounter had left me feeling strangely deflated and hollow. I usually enjoyed this sort of job. There was a strange sense of fulfilment in it, knowing you'd given a blind man a light to see with and shown him the path. It could even be fun smashing down their delusions of grandeur and importance.

There wasn't any fun in threatening old and desperate men.

In New York, this had never been a problem. Don DeCampo had never lent a man more than he could afford to borrow, and if some fool had got himself so deep in the red, he would come begging the Don for a favour. It had always been so easy to settle. No money lender would dare refuse the Don, for fear me and my brother would come to his door one night to make him see sense.

But here, there were no civilised rules. Men like Mr Ritter would lend money to anyone, and then came to me to get it back. As if I could get blood from a stone.

"Please. I just need more time…" Riley's desperate plea haunted my steps.

I might as well have been a thug with a bat.

My threat had been strong, but necessary. Riley thought he couldn't do it. If you thought you couldn't do something, you wouldn't try, but put the fear into a man, make him desperate, and he could do the impossible. It worked, but that didn't mean I had to like it.

Well, Riley was scared now. I just had to hope he didn't disappoint me. Or I'd be obliged to break his legs.

After all, a man was only as good as his word.

Don DeCampo had been particularly fond of that expression and had drilled that lesson into his *sons*. He had always said, all we have in this world is our word and our balls. Without this, we are little more than beasts and *Russians*.

At the thought of Russians, my thoughts jumped back to the events at the Beached Whale, and my stomach gave a conspicuous rumble as I pictured my unfinished burger on the table. I couldn't help but grin at the thought of what that girl might do if I turned up to collect the doggy bag.

It was true what they said. You really shouldn't shit where you eat.

They'd probably let me back in after a few weeks, once everything had blown over. Debra might even put in a good word for me. She'd seen everything after all and knew I wasn't usually trouble, but for now I'd best play it safe and stay scarce. Discretion was the better part of valour after all, and I had enough on my plate without Roy and his mates looking for a rematch.

Warm light from the street lamps burned up ahead as the road curved around and down between Wild Frontiers and whatever store was next door, emerging out into the car park. Following the sidewalk, I looked up, saw the broad body of a silhouette walking the other way, and froze.

I felt like I was back there, that night, in my bedroom above my parents' shop in Brighton Beach, all those years ago. Once again, those icy fingers crept down my spine, just as they had when the monster came to my door.

Sabor!

The name was on my lips before I could dismiss it. Sabor was long dead. I had killed him five years ago. Anyway, this body was also far too short. Alexi's favourite enforcer had been a giant and an enormous beast of a man, all muscle and tattoos. No, it couldn't be him. But then why did I have this feeling like I was a deer? A deer that had just seen the hounds come bounding out of the bush at the hunter's whistle.

Head down, I pushed on through the sudden discomfort and kept moving, yet I couldn't help glancing around. No new cars on site, so where the fuck had this guy come from? And where was he going? No bags in hand, so he wasn't out for a bit of evening shopping, and he certainly wasn't dressed for an evening stroll. That fancy overcoat would certainly keep the worst of any chill off, but under it he wore a tailored three-piece suit. A high end tailor too, the sort you find on Savile Row, not the joint along Port Angeles main that would cut your keys for you while you wait.

There was something else, too. His movements weren't right. There was just something about the way he walked as he stalked closer to me. It didn't suit him. Like he was restraining himself, preparing, but preparing for what?

I shifted focus to his face as I drew closer, hard jaw rough with a few days' growth, dark hair cut short, pale skin and Slavic features. He was looking my way, but his eyes, a hard ice blue even in the low light from the nearby streetlamps, were not on me. Watching, but not looking, careful not to hint what he was about to–fuck!

I didn't know this man. He didn't have any distinguishing features or markings I recognised. He could have been anyone from anywhere. Yet the one most important lesson life can teach is to trust that little voice in the back of our heads. Mine had saved my life more than once, and now it was screaming at me to get the hell out of dodge. This guy was a player. A Russian player, and I'd been made.

Only it was way too late for me to do anything about it.

Shit! Could this be one of Alexi's men? No, Alexi would have sent a hit team. After what I'd done to his men last time, he would have wanted to make sure he got me, but if not Alexi, then who?

Careful to keep my movements slow, I balled both hands into fists, steeling myself to strike. This would need to be done quickly and in close quarters. Move too soon and he could throw down. Just because he didn't look like he was carrying didn't mean he wasn't. That coat could easily conceal the bulge of a holster. That thought made me remember the gear I had stashed away at the barn, and my newly acquired knife sitting just over there in the door of the 911. All safely stored and of no use to me.

I'd really dropped a bollock this time.

Then the moment to act came and we were all but eye to eye. I steeled myself for the blow I knew was about to come, ready to return the favour with one of my own. Then his eyes flicked back to meet mine and instead, he and his overcoat veered to my right, casually stepping around me and kept on walking. I heard his footsteps tapping on the pavement, falling away into silence. It took all my willpower to resist the urge to look back. Instead, I forced myself to just keep walking like nothing had happened. Even so, I couldn't help letting out a breath. Only when I got back to the 911 did I risk a glance backward and could just make out his form, still walking in the same direction.

"What the fuck was his problem?" I mused, climbing back into the car. I put a hand down to the knife in the door, as much to settle the screaming voice inside my head as reassure myself it was still there. It didn't help, and I decided it was time to kick silver into gear and do the banana trick and split.

Then a fresh rumble from my stomach reminded me of my other pressing problem. So, I took a detour route home, via the Walmart Superstore just down the 101.

I didn't need much. I wasn't exactly what you'd call a gourmet chef and always favoured eating out to cooking for myself. It wasn't as if Port Angeles was exactly lacking in restaurants after all, and plenty would deliver. Still, you don't always get a choice in the matter. When it was near nine and everywhere would more than likely be full, your guts would sing up like Pavarotti's greatest hits. Beggars definitely couldn't be choosers.

It was a big place. Huge compared to the ones I'd occasionally seen in New York, where space came at a premium and the locals knew how to pack everything and the kitchen sink into a carry-on bag. It was blessedly quiet, with only a handful of cars in the lot and not quite as many staff behind the tills and walking the floor.

Grabbing a basket, my first point of call was the fruit and veg for some tomatoes and mushrooms. Then into the fridge section for a pack of bacon and a few chipolatas, though I skipped the black pudding. A pack of six eggs and a loaf of bread landed in the basket after a walk along the back wall. Almost done, all I needed was to pick up a can of baked beans on my way to the tills and I'd be off, homeward bound for a proper Full English.

Simple enough, unless you had 'mug' stamped across your forehead.

I'd just collected my can of Heinz and was rounding the bend with my basket in hand, about to pay for my groceries, when I saw a woman down the next aisle. She was standing on the tips of her flat canvas shoes with her back to me, trying to reach something on the top shelf. A small thing, with rich dark hair that tumbled down her back, dressed in a faded denim jacket and jeans.

On any other day, I'd have probably left her to it. People just didn't help each other anymore, and I wasn't any different. I never claimed to be Sir Galahad. In fact, I was worse. I wanted to stay under the radar, and the way to do that was by being invisible. In my old life, reputation was everything. I had been a man of reputation, and my esteemed reputation had always preceded me. My death had given me a fresh start, but start helping every Tom, Dick, and Harriet that you crossed, and you would get noticed. If people started noticing me, eventually that reputation would come back to haunt me. That didn't mean I wouldn't hold a door open for someone when our paths crossed, though. That was just rude, which could be just as counterproductive.

The trick was just to never go out of my way.

She was halfway down an aisle that I had absolutely no reason to go down. I'd never had much of a sweet tooth and confectionery wasn't my style. However, I was still feeling pretty shitty after threatening to break Riley's legs and wanted to do something to make myself feel better.

"Here, let me get that for you," I say, not even bothering to ask as I came up behind her, reached over her head and grabbed the bag of sweets.

"Oh, thank you very much," she said, twisting to face me, a broad, grateful smile spreading across her lips as I handed her the candy, which promptly dropped when she saw my face.

Her eyes went wide.

"You!"

Shit!

Chapter Four

Well now, what would be the odds of this? How would Humphrey Bogart have put it? Of all the aisles in all the Walmarts in the state, I just had to walk into hers.

The girl from the Beached Whale just glowered, her eyes wide and disbelieving, and I couldn't help but grin. "Me."

She looked even more beautiful up close, and this angle offered a tantalizing glimpse down the V-neck of her top to the swells of her breasts. Yet it was her eyes that grabbed me. They were such a beautiful shade of blue, as deep clear as the ocean. Yet there was something else. Something very familiar about them. I'd seen them before somewhere, I was sure of it, but where?

However, the look blazing in those fierce, Icey waters suggested she didn't see the funny side of this serendipitous moment quite the way I did. "What-what are you doing here? Are you following me?"

"Following you?" I could help but laugh. "Now, why would I be doing that?"

She hadn't struck me as the type to be that full of herself. Then again, if I'd been in her shoes, and bumped into the punter from my work, who'd just fucked up a group of Russians for me, in a supermarket halfway across the county, I guess I'd have been a tad suspicious too.

She looked like she wanted to say just why she thought I was following her, and probably wouldn't have been too shy about expressing herself in some very colourful terms. Then she must have thought better of it, as I'd already shown I wasn't worried about expressing my own views in public. Of course, she would never have been in any danger around me. It might have been old fashioned and rather sexist in this liberal world, but I had never hit girls.

"Never mind, it doesn't matter," she growled, dropping the bag of candy into the basket by her feet. The only other item in there was a microwave meal that was probably about as nutritious as the box it came in and had only a day or two left on the use by date. "What are you doing here, then?"

"Shopping. Same as you." I held up my much fuller basket for her to see. "I fancied a full English tonight."

"A what?" She arched a brow, her suspicious look melting away for a moment, to one of genuine bewilderment that looked very cute on her.

I couldn't resist the opening. "Full English, you know? Bacon, sausage, eggs, beans, mushrooms and tomatoes with a few rounds of toast. A full English Breakfast."

"But it's too late for breakfast." Her nose practically wrinkled at the implication.

"Not in Australia, love," I teased. "And in England, any time is a good time for a fry up."

"Sounds delightful." Her tone dripped with sarcasm, and I swear I'd never been so tempted to swat an ass in my life. She definitely had a butt made to be slapped, or squeezed, or framed and hung in the Louvre. Clad in those denim jeans, it was a certifiable work of art.

"Ah, don't knock it till you try it. This will cure anything, from a hangover to a broken heart," I promised, knowing I must have sounded like a salesperson on an infomercial, but the words were out before I could stop them.

The line was one of my old man's. He'd always sworn by it, even when my mum was telling him a doctor would disagree. He'd just say, "And a Doctor told Snow White she needed to eat more fruit, and look what happened to that old cow." She'd laugh at that, and then it would all be good between them. But by the look on her face, this girl wasn't about to give me the same opening. Pity, I'd rather like to see her smile again. "So, does your boss know you're doing a grocery run on company time?"

I reckoned she should have had at least another hour left of her shift at the Beached Whale. Hospitality work was the same the world over- long hours for shit pay. It didn't matter if it was in a greasy spoon or Gordon Ramsey's next bistro. If you came in on the afternoon shift, you'd be doing the cleanup after shutting up. And there was still another hour or two before the Beached Whale rang the bell for the last call.

"Oh-that's none of your -oh, whatever, just leave me alone will you, alright?" she snapped, grabbing the candy from her basket and throwing it at my face before turning on her heel. There was an unmistakable catch to her voice as she shot back. "Why don't you just fuck off! You've ruined my life enough for one day…"

She had made it barely four strides when I touched a hand to her shoulder to stop her. She tried to shrug me off, but I'd already stepped around her to block her way. "Hey, what's wrong?"

"They fired me alright!" she sobbed, her eyes sparkling with tears, like a sea of diamonds. "I got fired because of you and your macho bullshit!"

I blinked and raised my hands defensively. "Me? What did I do?"

What was this girl on about? How could I be responsible for her getting the sack?

"That fight, you idiot!" she exclaimed, stabbing me in the chest with her finger. "When the boss came in to find out what happened, *Marcus* blamed me. Said I'd been giving those men the runaround, and you were drunk and got jealous, and started a bar fight before taking off."

"The fight?" I asked. I knew I must have sounded like I'd taken one too many kicks to the head, but I didn't give a shit. This made no sense. It was insane. Then her words sunk in and I remembered the barman and I had the sudden urge to wring the little shit's neck. "And what, he just took that limp dick's word for it?"

Her eyes almost did a full 360 in their sockets. "Of course he did. He's his son. I tried telling him what happened, but he just said he should have known better than to hire an Indian bitch and told me to take a hike and not to bother asking for a reference." And with that, whatever damn inside her that was holding back the tears broke apart, and she sobbed. "I needed that job, asshole! Now, what am I going to do? Do you know how hard it is to find work in this town?"

And I had no fucking idea what to do.

I didn't know how to comfort a crying girl.

I'd never been what people called an emotional person. It just wasn't in my nature. Never had been. When I'd been in the system, one of my foster families had been concerned about my refusal to open up and 'talk about what had happened, and all I must have been going through.' They'd even taken me to see a child shrink who'd diagnosed me with just about everything from PTSD to emotional withdrawal. He must have just loved reading my file and imagining all my possible conditions that he'd charge by the hour for. I bet he'd offered them counselling after I ran away. Then again, they had probably needed it more than I had.

I wasn't a head case. I'd just never needed to talk it through.

I'd just found healthier ways of dealing with it.

Revenge didn't solve problems. It didn't fix what was broken. However, the idea of it gave me something else to think about, something to focus on, and you know what, when the moment came, it actually felt rather good.

Not as good as I'd hoped. Still, it beat listening to Dr Sigmund Fraud explain how my nightmares were rooted in my Oedipus desire to fuck my foster mother.

I wonder if she'd been thinking about it too. Just driving around, hoping I might cross the road in front of her so she could run me down like Bruce Willis in Pulp Fiction.

I stepped forward, trying to put a comforting hand around her. It always worked in the movies, right? "I'm sorry, I didn't realise, I was just trying to-"

She prodded a finger into my chest. "What? You think I can't handle myself? All you had to do was stay out of it. They would have got bored and left, but now? What am I going to do?"

She just stared at me. The tears still coming, but past them, her eyes burned with a mix of naked fury and outrage and just a simple need for an answer. An answer I didn't have. I didn't know what to say. What could I say to make it all make sense?

'Suck it up', or, 'that's life?' Somehow, I got the feeling that wouldn't help very much.

Of course, it wasn't right or fair, but that was the way of the world. The strong prey on the weak. The powerful prosper, while the helpless and vulnerable get fucked over. I'd seen it every day. It was the law of the jungle. Sometimes I was a powerful hunter, and sometimes I was prey. You took the knocks as they came, dealt with them, then moved on. You had to be practical about these things, though that never made them any easier to bear.

But this was different.

Guilt tore at my insides, wrapping around me like the coils of a great ice serpent intent on devouring me from the inside out.

This wasn't one of life's sadistic chance cards. This was my fault. I'd done this to her, and that idea grounded me. I wanted to help, to make it right. And I could. So I would.

I shook my head and dropped my basket on the floor. "Nothing, you're not fired. Don't worry."

She blinked. "What-what do you mean?"

"You lost your job on my account. Nope, sorry, I can't live with that. You just go home, have your sweets, and in the morning, your boss will call you and everything will be right with the world. Don't worry, I'll take care of everything," I promised, turning my back on her.

"Oh yeah, and how are you going to do that?" she shouted after me.

Yeah, Sherlock, just how are you going to do it? I didn't really have an answer for her.

"I'm gonna make him an offer he can't refuse." The words were out of my mouth before I could stop them.

Guess it could have been worse. At least I didn't say something cliché, like 'Don't ask me about my business.'

That might have given her the wrong idea.

There is an old expression in prizefighting-everyone's got a plan until they're hit. It's why I had always preferred to make it up as I go. A lot of wise and learned men have excelled in the virtues of planning from behind their desks, but never really took into account what to do when the opposition did something that wasn't in the script. Better just to know where you want to go, and not worry about every fork in the road.

That's why, when I slid the 911 back into the Beached Whale's car park and saw it empty for all but the old Ford pickup and a black Suburban with tinted windows pulled up outside the door, I didn't start flapping. Though the big guy standing outside the door did little to improve my prospects.

Was he here because of the fight? Had the owner decided to pony up the cash to hire a doorman to keep undesirables, namely me, out?

I kind of doubted that. If every bar started hiring that sort of muscle whenever there was a fight, muscle work would be one of the country's top growth industries, but you never know.

Or, of course, there was the other option, and my friends were back.

Cliché car out front. Big brick shithouse almost as big as the door he was guarding, with a buzz cut and more ink on his skin than in a tattoo shop window, dressed in a cheap overcoat that didn't quite hide the bulk over the holster under his arm. Put all that together and it meant only one thing in my experience.

Still, only one way to find out.

The big guy watched with undisguised hostility as I pulled the Porsche into a space a few spots down from the Suburban. Killing the engine, I was halfway out of the door, then thought better of it and reached down to the side compartment and pulled out the knife. Careful to keep it out of sight of the gorilla by the door, I strapped it to my belt, gave it a shake to make sure the blade wouldn't get caught on the draw, then pulled my jacket back on, hiding the blade from sight.

I wouldn't walk in there looking for a fight, but if shit hits the fan, it would be better to have a blade and not need it than to need it and not have one.

Much like a condom.

"Bar's closed," the big guy grunted as I approached, and I could have sworn on the spot. Great, fucking Russians again. I knew it.

Someone give me a goddamn PHD or my own psychic hotline.

And this guy wasn't some American born, second generation Russian American like Roy and his mates. This guy's accent was Russian through and through, a variant of Muscovite, but from the rough side of the city. The Moscow equivalent of South London, but without the charm. He must be the muscle the boss flew in from the old country.

Yeah, this really wasn't my day.

"Really?" I ask, quickly using my bad American accent to play the part of stupid yuppy that can't take a hint. Then, checking my watch, I added. "It's only nine-thirty."

"Closed," he growled, in a way that seriously gave off the Arnold Schwarzenegger vibe from Red Heat. Or maybe it was just the way he was glaring down at me that gave the impression he was considering ripping my leg off to see if I had a couple of keys of coke stashed up there.

Undaunted, but keeping to character, I injected a bit of a tremor into my voice as I nodded to the bright red neon sign in the window. "Sign says open."

"Sign Broken. Bar closed," he hawked, then spat a dark glob of phlegm on the ground, just missing my shoes, before bending so our faces were close enough for him to exhale a cloud of vodka and Russian tobacco smoke on my face. "And if you don't fuck off, I am going to fuck you up like the little bitch you-"

The malice in his threat dissolved into a fit of choked wheezing as I rammed the cradle of my right hand up into his exposed larynx. It wasn't a crippling strike. For all the damage inflicted in the movies, unless you pulled a Patrick Swayze and got sufficient purchase to rip the throat out, the larynx is a very sturdy, elastic muscle. The moment the hand is pulled back, it'll just spring back into place like it never happened.

But that sensation of suddenly having the windpipe jammed shut, like an invisible fist had closed around your throat and was squeezing hard? That was as bad as it got.

If you could just shrug it off and throw it down, you were doing bloody well.

This guy didn't do so well. Unprepared for the sucker punch, no sooner had I pulled my hand back than his hands were clawing at the invisible noose in a mad, desperate panic.

And as he struggled, all my instincts screamed at me to take my knife and end his miserable life. I would have done it once, if our paths had crossed in NYC, back in the good old days. I'd have taken the steel and buried it in his eye and then left him in the street as a warning to all who would dare cross the DeCampos. A reminder that their white ape, their most feared enforcer, the Tarzan of New York, showed no mercy.

But that man was dead.

He died five years ago. Executed by his big brother before the most feared Pakhan in all the Americas. His corpse, dumped into the river to feed the fish and eels. It had been the price of peace, and for that reason, he would stay dead.

So instead, I grabbed his head and smashed it sideways into the brick wall, hard enough to send chunks of masonry flying like shattered china. He slumped down after them, alive but unquestionably

unconscious, and with the mother of all headaches
waiting for him when he woke up.

Stooping down onto one knee, I leaned over him
and I reached into his coat, felt the cool of textured
pistol grip, and pulled out a classic. A Beretta 92.

"Oh, this is very bad for you," I told the
unconscious goon, before ejecting the mag, racking
the slider to clear the chamber and giving it a quick
rub down with my shirt to remove any fingerprints.
Then I drew back my bowling arm and hurled it
around and sent it spinning end over end, across the
car park and over the cliff edge, down into the dark
depths of the straight.

Never use a strange gun. It was the golden rule of
firearms.

If the cops caught you with it, and could link it to
any crime, anywhere, they'd pin it on you and not let
a silly little thing like innocence get in the way. Even
if you had an ironclad alibi. Even if you were lucky
enough to be caught enjoying a ménage à trois
between Kate Beckinsale and Madison Ivy, and a
photo of it was doing the rounds in every
supermarket tabloid and celebrity blog out there with
a timestamp detailing the exact time and date of the
crime in question, they'd then just charge you as an
accessory. In either case, depending on the potluck of
crimes, it could cost you anything from five months to
a couple of lifetimes.

Hell of a price to pay for carelessness.

Long story short, if the piece wasn't untraceable or cleaner than a vestal virgin, I wouldn't touch it.

And I certainly would not leave it with the sleeping goon here. With the way my luck was going today, he would probably come around as I was leaving and give me another hole to breathe out of.

With his gun out of the question, I quickly rolled him onto his back and patted him down, but only found a set of car keys and a wallet. Looks like someone wasn't a part of the Stalin Youth. The wallet contained an American Express, $250 in cash, and a fake ID that must have cost a fortune. I couldn't tell it was fake from looking at it, but not even Muscovites were cruel enough to call their kid Brooklyn Kennedy.

It was an excellent picture, though. Had all the right government markings. Even the paper felt right. Definitely not the sort of thing you'd pick up from the back of a dodgy pawn shop. Would definitely pass muster with any bank teller or post office clerk until Brooklyn Kennedy started gobbing off or scribbled his John Hancock in Cyrillic handwriting. Then they might just twig it.

Returning the wallet and keys, minus the $250 which I took as compensation, I left him there and instead just stepped over him. It would have taken too long to move him and there was no point restraining him. After a hit like that, he wouldn't be going anywhere on his own for a while.

Inside, the Whale looked much as it had done before my earlier visit. The tables had been rearranged and there was no trace of broken glass. Even the pool cue was back atop the table. It could have passed for any other bar on a Monday night, except that it was almost entirely deserted for all but four guys around the bar, and I somehow doubted they were here for the burgers.

I recognised two of them.

The first was the owner of the bar. Ned Gates, a fat little grease ball with blanched skin, sunken eyes, and slick, oiled, dark hair who always came to the bar dressed in bright gaudy suites that struggled to contain his barreled chest. He looked like he was trying too hard to emulate Robert DeNiro, but ended up giving off John Cazale vibes.

The other guy was Roy, who had Ned laid out across the bar with a hand to his throat. A younger dude I hadn't seen earlier was behind the bar, bent down and telling Gates something. I couldn't hear what he was saying, but it twisted his mouth in a rictus of a grin and his head was bobbing like one of those dog ornaments I'd seen on car dashboards. He must have spent an hour a day styling his floppy brown hair.

The fourth guy was off to the side. Tall and so straight-backed he could easily have had a cane shoved up his arse. He might have been middle-aged, but there were no visible tattoos and his dark hair and goatee were neatly trimmed without a hint of grey.

He wore a medallion of an old Russian saint around his neck, probably Vasily the Blessed, the saint that could inspire fear and respect amongst the powerful, and a favourite amongst the Bratva. This must have been the boss. That suit and tie were very middle of the road, definitely not Savile Row, but not off the rack either. Sharp with a good tailored fit. Not the sort of thing a foot soldier would wear. One of Roy's friends, as he'd put it. Not bloody likely. This guy would have even fewer friends than I did, and that was saying something.

He was obviously a brigadier, or *Avtoritet*. A captain. This guy would live for his brotherhood and the Pakhan, his every instinct set towards climbing the Bratva political ladder.

Which explained why he was paying a visit. Some of his soldiers took a beating on the premises. Now an example had to be made. Or else his group would look weak. He would look weak.

Which meant one of us was about to have a very bad night.

"Hello," I announced, forcing a grin as all eyes in the room suddenly locked on me. "Oh sorry, am I interrupting?"

The suit rounded on me, spitting with all the pompous fury that could only come from mother Russia. "Can't you see we're fucking closed? Get out of here! Boris, Boris, get your fucking ass in here!"

"Boris is taking a little nap," I said, hoping he meant the big boy counting sheep outside. "Poor bloke. Looks like he's been banging his head against a wall, so I told him I'd take over."

The suit snorted, colour rushing to his face. "You'd take over? You'd take fucking over? Yobanaya suka!" Behind him, Roy and his mate left Ned on the bar to fall in. He wasn't their problem anymore and by the look of the ugly purple swelling across his face, they hadn't left him in much of a state to cause them any trouble. "Go! Get the fuck out, before I cut your fucking balls off and feed them to you like *Pelmeni*!"

"Now, that's not very nice." I gave them a boyish grin, like the schoolboy that knew he was getting to his schoolmaster, keeping my hands low and ready to draw my blade, careful not to make any quick movements. If Boris was packing, they would be too. I had to wait for them to get in close. I'd never had Pelmeni, and if my balls were going to be my introduction, I sure as hell wasn't in the mood for it tonight.

Roy's mate grinned as they moved around the tables on either side. "You hear this bitch? 'Not very nice', I'll show you not very nice-"

"Hey boss, wait, that's the guy!" Roy broke in, his eyes going wide as he came in close enough to get a better look at my face. I could see him too, and it was obvious which of us came off worse. My cheek had been throbbing with what could have been the start of a shiner, but he looked almost as bad as that sack of meat on the table. You could also hear the improvements his missing teeth had done to his voice.

The *Avtoritet* rounded on Roy, his face a mix of disgust and astonishment. "*That's* the guy?"

"Yeah, that's him." Roy's hand edged to his holstered piece, pausing just on the edge of his jacket, fingers flexing with the itch to throw down. "He's quicker than he looks," he snarled, his eyes burning with hate, yet didn't take another step. He wanted to kill me. He knew he should, but he also needed to break me. I'd beaten him, humiliated him. Now he needed to redeem himself to his boss, to show he was still a man to fear, a man worthy of the brotherhood.

Or else he was out.

And the brotherhood was a lifelong commitment. There was only one way out.

He was quite literally between a rock and a hard place.

Take his swift revenge here, be regarded as a coward by his brotherhood, and face being condemned excommunicado. Or try to redeem himself and face another beating.

His mate wasn't so cautious. "You gotta be fucking joking? This little bitch?"

"Yeah," Roy grunted, and I could see the monkeys in his head beating each other with sticks. He wanted this guy to have a go at me as he had. Then, as I dealt with him, he would have carte blanche to put me down, *'to protect his brother'*.

"I don't believe it," Floppy-hair drawled, coming in close enough for spittle to rain down on my cheek as he asked, "Who are you?"

This punk had obviously been playing a bit too much Grand Theft Auto.

Young and stupid, eager to please and show off how tough he was. I knew the type well enough, and had seen more than my fair share. Every young punk who had ever joined a gang was just like this. It didn't matter if they were Bratva or Cosa Nostra, Triad, Yakuza, Cartel Gangbanger or just wannabe gangsters, they were all the same. Fresh meat for the grinder. Most wound up dead or in jail within a year or two if they didn't get seasoned quickly.

It would have been the easiest thing in the world to put him down. He was so close, I could have drawn the blade and lodged it in his heart before he ever knew he was dead, but Roy would start shooting and I wasn't sure I could get to him before he filled me so full of lead, they could have sharpened my head for a pencil. Instead, I forced down the urge and kept grinning. "Apparently I'm the guy."

I tensed, ready to take the hit I expected to follow, but the guy's grin just twisted even wider, an ugly sneer of barbed wire. He turned to the suit. "You want me to handle him for you, *Brigadier*?"

"Net, Dodolzksi, you couldn't handle a wet dream. Now get back and shut the fuck up." It obviously wasn't the answer the youth had wanted because his grin dropped, but he obediently stepped back around the nearest table. The Brigadier, or Avtoritet, meaning one with authority, as they were sometimes known, turned to me, his expression set and unreadable behind the black predatory eyes of a weasel. "Did you do this thing?"

Of the three, this was the man to fear.

He had probably about ten years on me, old enough to have experience but not too old to have lost his edge. He stood straight but easy, ready to spring like a cat in a tree. That told me he was a fighter from the street. The sons and brothers of high ranked members of the brotherhood, who got handed positions of power, never lost the swagger that came from knowing they had friends in high places and would strut about like peacocks. This guy was a soldier. A fighter. An animal who'd learned to live by the laws of the concrete jungle, and he knew the kind when he saw it.

"What thing?" I shrugged, playing dumb, needing to piss him off some more, provoke him into becoming reckless.

Something dangerous flashed behind his eyes, but the suit had an older man's control and buried it down. "Assaulted my boys."

He knew my game, as I knew his. We were both old hands at this. The only question was, who would break first? "Oh, that thing." I shrugged again and inclined my head across the opposite table to where my old mate Roy was trying to circle around behind me. "Roy over there backwashed my coke. So I gave him a lesson in manners. The others disagreed with my teaching methods. So I explained my point."

"A lesson in manners?" The suit repeated slowly, his tone even with a deadly purpose. Yet his eye twitched.

Sensing the chink in his armour, the aggression radiating off him; I pressed. Russians were, after all, a famously excitable race. "Yeah. And they were slow learners."

That twitch again, and this time his mouth curled dangerously.

Unfortunately, the suit wasn't the only Russian in the room.

American born or not, Roy was as hot-blooded as any of his countrymen. Red faced, he threw a desperate look at his Brigadier. "He's lying Mikhail, we were-"

"Now, didn't we have a little conversation earlier about that mouth of yours?" I barked, my voice even but suddenly hard with intent and an edge sharper than ice. Roy twisted back to look at me, his eyes black with hate, yet when our gazes met, he couldn't help but look away. I kept my gaze hard on him regardless, wanting him to remember my words and the promise of pain to follow if he interrupted me again. "So why don't you just shut up like a good gentleman, while you can still enjoy steak." There was murder in his eyes at that, and if he was going to shoot me, it would have been then. Inwardly, I prepared myself to dive behind the tables, but he must've been sufficiently cowed because his hand stayed where it was. Forcing my boyish grin back into place, I turned back to the suit, who I guessed was called Mikhail. "See what I mean, slow learners. But they can be taught."

"So, what are you doing here now?" Mikhail growled softly, dangerously, the insult about his men rankling more than if my threat had been directed at him.

I shrugged as if it was of no importance. "Well, I was just doing a bit of shopping when I ran into the waitress that had been serving us. Poor thing was in tears. Seems that Mr Gates over there blamed her for the whole thing, even fired her for it."

"Oh, really?" he asked, with only the barest hint of interest, as if he were examining an ant crossing a table, before crushing it.

"Aww, don't it just break your heart," Dodolzksi said in a sing song fashion, mocking me openly, circling around the tables to stand just out of reach.

I didn't rise to the bait.

Pretending not to have noticed the other man, I stared hard at the suit. "So I told her I'd get her job back and just came back to complain. Only I can't do that with you boys hog-tying him to the bar and spit roasting him like one of your two-dollar gimps, now can I? So why don't you pop off and boil an egg, I'll only be a minute."

If that didn't get him riled, nothing would.

Life had taught me there were three simple truths about Russians you could set your watch to.

They loved their vodka.

They were as excitable as a bunch of four-year-olds in a sweet shop.

And the whole damn nation was as homophobic as a sainted Texan bishop.

"Go boil an egg…" Mikhail parroted, testing the words in his mouth, before throwing back his head and laughing a cruel barking cough that was as hard as nails on a chalkboard. "That is a funny guy over there."

Then the moment passed. His laughter went silent and there was only the cold mercilessness in his predator's eyes. "Alright, so what's gonna happen is you're gonna come along with us, funny guy, and we're gonna talk about this lesson you gave my boys." He motioned to Roy and his mate. "Take him."

It was the signal the pair had been waiting for. Like well-trained dogs, they surged around the table to seize me, rough hands grabbing and twisting my arms behind my back.

"Come along, Mr funny man," Dodolzksi instructed in that singsong voice, his gaping grin as wide and bright as an angel's halo as he tugged me along towards the door.

"Yeah, it's time we revisit your earlier remarks," Roy snarled. His courage returned with his partner's enthusiasm.

I didn't resist and let them lead me. "What? Hey wait, come on guys, let's just talk about this, okay, have you heard this joke? You'll love this, I promise. So this bloke walks into a pub with his little dog under his arm. Goes up and sets the dog down on the bar before sitting down. The barman looks on, thinking what the fuck is going on here, and to his surprise the dog turns around and-" I lurched sideways, smashing the side of my skull into Roy's battered face.

Bone met bone with a vicious crack, and Roy was sent reeling. Dodolzksi must have felt my body tense in preparation, because he was already trying to pull me back. However, that was just what I wanted from him. As Roy went down, his hold on me went slack and I was free to pivot into the younger man as he pulled me into him. I had just enough time to tuck my chin in before head-butting him hard enough for stars to burst before my eyes.

I caught the briefest glimpse of Dodolzksi slumped against a table, both hands up to his face, trying to stem the blood squirting through his fingers from a probably broken nose. Then I was moving again, barrelling through and over tables, charging at Mikhail.

His eyes went wide as he saw me coming at him, but an old soldier through and through, he reacted, his body shifting, lowering into a fighting stance. He expected me to launch a head on attack, so his hand cranked back, and he stepped in to deliver one of his own.

And that was his mistake.

The punch came in swinging hard and fast, but I was already moving, sidestepping out of the way, and as I did, my hand snaked out to grab his tie. Then I was twisting, bringing it up and over his shoulder, then down into the nearest table. In an instant, the knife sheathed at my back was in my hand, and I buried the blade down through the tie while driving my heel back into the rear of his knee.

The effect was immediate. His whole body dropped like a sack of potatoes. The tie snapped tight like a hangman rope and his feet, dressed in Oxford's polished to a high shine, started drumming up the hangman's jig while he clawed at the knot. It would do no good. Silk under tension was as non-pliable as it was unbreakable. He was stuck there, strangled by his own tie, eyes wide and bulging as I reached into his jacket and took his weapon from its holster.

It was a fifth generation Glock 17.

Unimaginative, but a good, reliable weapon, and expensive. So expensive, it almost tempted me to break the first rule and keep it as a souvenir.

Something big and heavy collided with my back, knocking the pistol skidded out of my hands. Then an arm slid around my neck, dragging my head back, while the other pawed at my arm, trying to hook it behind my back.

Dodolzksi.

Resisting the flare of panic as I struggled to breathe through the heady mix of tobacco smoke, onions, and blood, I reached back and grabbed the arm around my throat by the shoulder. Not so much trying to pull it away, but to draw the younger man closer so I could drive my other arm back, jabbing my elbow into his body. He grunted out as the hits made contact once, twice, then thrice, but he held on regardless, stubborn as a Jack Russell dangling from an old sock. And I knew why.

Out of the corner of my eye, I glimpsed Roy advancing on us. He took his time, letting me see him and know he was coming for me. His pride would sting from his earlier beating, and he wanted revenge. If he was smart, he would have shot me there and then. But a bullet to the head wouldn't be enough to heal the wounds I'd dealt him.

He wanted true revenge.

This was his chance. I was trapped, restrained, barely able to fight back. Now he could tenderise me. Beat me to a pulp. Then the fun would begin, and he was feeling pretty cocky about it.

So cocky, he ended up walking straight into my kick.

Vinny Jones was right. You really couldn't underestimate the predictability of stupidity.

That first kick connected with his belly and produced a strangled, almost inaudible groan. My next smashed into the side of his knee and sent him to the floor. That second kick also gave me the brace I needed to drive Dodolzksi backward. No doubt surprised by the sudden jerk, he had no choice but to go with me, his arm loosening just enough for me to smash my head back into whatever was left of his nose.

His agonised scream came out loud and shrill, so close to my ears, but I was already twisting free of his hold, and the pain of my ringing ears only added extra ferocity to the hook as I smashed into the bloody mess of his face. He went down hard, landing atop a table that collapsed beneath the hit. He wouldn't be getting up from that in a hurry.

There was a noise behind me. A grunt. The rumble of a table grinding across the floor. I looked back in time to see Roy struggle to his feet, one arm braced against the nearest table, the other shoved beneath his jacket.

When his hand came out, it clasped the black shape of a Barretta.

I caught it just before he could bring it to bear, closing my hand around the barrel and twisting it up and away with his finger still on the trigger. Roy hissed out an agonised sound as the guard bent the finger at all the wrong angles. When I twisted it again, he threw his head back, and I brought my knee up to meet the bottom of his jaw. The force pulverised whatever teeth he had left.

No one could say I hadn't warned him.

"You really are a slow learner, aren't you?" I mused, more to myself than the mass writhing on the floor as I checked his gun, a fairly beaten up Beretta 92. Ejecting the mag, I quickly pocketed it before stooping down over Roy. "Look at me."

His eyes were glassy when he looked up and he seemed to struggle to focus through the pain, so I made sure he knew I meant business by stabbing the Barretta's muzzle into his groin.

I thumbed back the trigger. "I see your face again, and you'll wish I kept the mag in, crystal?"

He couldn't speak. Half his teeth were buried in the roof of his mouth. So he just nodded, with more enthusiasm than a man in his line of work should have given his position.

"Good," I smiled, then a thought occurred to me. "By the way, did you ever chamber the round?" He shook his head, but the movement was so fast, I couldn't quite tell if that was a no, or a yes. Maybe he didn't know. "Can't remember? Oh well, that's alright. These things happen. Let's find out."

His eyes widened, and he opened his mouth to scream as I pulled the trigger. But only the snap of the dead man's click came out.

"You lucky bastard." I dropped the gun to the floor between his legs. Out of courtesy, I pretended not to notice the dark stain spreading across his jeans, nor the acrid scent of piss rising from it. "Now get out of here before I change my mind and take your friend over there with you."

Roy didn't argue, just rolled over and forced himself to rise. Likewise, the bloodied mess that had been Dodolzksi, who had been watching the show, did as he was told, and together the pair scurried away with their tails between their legs.

I watched them go.

It would probably have been easier to kill them. They were in the underworld. They probably more than had it coming already. But even in that shadowy world of crime, death had a cost, and it was always messy. You couldn't just kill two people and walk away. In the movies, Keanu Reeves might be able to leave a trail of corpses across New York and not worry about repercussions, but things worked a little differently in real life. Bodies had to be disposed of, the crime scenes cleansed, and any witnesses *liquidated*. And if that wasn't an option, a fall guy had to be put in place, because the law would want an answer. That was unavoidable. A body meant the law, and even when they were on the take, they still had to present an answer to the crime to satisfy the public and make it all disappear. Unanswered crimes lived on forever, not only as a file in the cold case office, but as legend. An unsolved crime never went away, but give the public a face, a name, a villain to blame, and it all became just a matter of record.

Don DeCampo had been a master at working such things. He was the puppeteer, and the world danced to his strings, but I wasn't his man anymore. I couldn't pull a string, make a man an offer, and have him hold his hands up to multiple murders. I was on my own, and killing them meant I had to kill everyone here, then burn the site down, then kill that girl, as she was the only other person who knew I was here.

That was what it took to get away with murder, and I had never been that kind of man. The girl was innocent. She wasn't stained by the underworld's darkness. If I took her life, then I'd be no better than the man that had murdered my parents.

So I let them go, and instead turned back to Mikhail.

He'd managed to get his footing, but his face had turned that dull shade of blue and red you normally only saw on a beetroot as he held on to his necktie with a death grip.

Walking up to him, I pulled out the nearest chair, turned it around and sat down, reverse style, with both hands folded atop the backrest. "Now, while you're just hanging there, pay attention, there's a good chap. Because I don't think anyone really wants what just happened here to get out. I doubt the knowledge that you and your boys got a good hiding twice in one day by the same man will do your business interest's any good. Nod if you agree."

He didn't respond, just glared daggers at me, so I stretched out a leg and started tapping my foot against his heel.

One kick and he'd be back to dancing the dead man's jig. "Nod." With a pleading, desperate sound rising in his throat, he started bobbing his head like he couldn't do it fast enough.

"Good. So there's no need for this to get out. You don't know me, and I don't know you, or who you work for. So, as far as the rest of the world is concerned, what happened here today never happened. It was just another series of bar fights in a cheap bar that sells bad beer and good burgers. And we all can go on with our lives like we never met. Do you agree?" This time he didn't need any prompting to nod, but the motion was so resentful, it tempted me to kick the leg out from under him on principle.

Instead, I got up out of the chair. "See, we can be civilised. Now get out." Walking around behind him, I wrenched the knife from the table and watched the suit promptly fall on his arse. Coughing violently, he scrambled back up to his full height, his face quickly reddening as blood returned to his head, murder burning in his eyes.

I didn't back down. Instead, I held his gaze until, with a muttered curse, he straightened out his suit lapels and turned away. When he was about to step out into the night, I called out, "By the way, next time you want to get a guy to talk, just cut off one of his pinky fingers. Then tell him his thumb's next. After that, he'll pretty much tell you whatever you want to know. Saves a lot of time."

Freezing mid-step, he shot me a glare back across his shoulder. "I'll see you later, funny man," he promised, his voice low and seething with barely leashed anger, before disappearing into the night.

"I can't wait," I mused before looking down at Gates. He looked even worse this close, like a raw steak that had been well and truly tenderized by Mike Tyson and Nick Fury. "You know, I don't know what it is about me today. I just keep getting into fights. I don't know, what do you think, is it my face?"

He groaned, his voice weak and barely coherent. "What do you want?"

"Now is that any way to say thank you?"

"Thank you," he asked slowly, his eyes slowly coming back into focus. "For what? You're the reason they did this to me." His voice was coming back, thick and passionate with that contentious mix of self-pity and accusation.

"I'm also the reason you came out of it with nothing more than a beating," I countered, my tone matter of fact, almost conversational. "You don't want to know what those boys would do once they'd have got started. If you'd been lucky, they would have just kneecapped you and left it as a message. But often as not, they'd take you to some deserted warehouse somewhere and give you a seeing to with baseball bats before leaving you a couple of days. Then when you're feeling good and sorry for yourself, they would come back, only they'd arrive with your wife or children in tow and make you watch as they-"

"Alright, alright, I get the picture," he groaned, the visual already too much. "Thank you," he spat it out with all the appreciation of a vegan in McDonald's before rolling up into a seated position. "What the hell do you want?"

"Like I told our mutual friends back there, I want you to give that girl her job back," I said, crossing my arms over my chest, bored with these games for one day.

His eyes went wide, and he struggled to think of something to say. "But she- she."

I wouldn't have it. We both knew the truth. She was disposable labour, easy to get rid of. Easier to just give her the boot than face the consequences of his nepotism.

"She's a sweet girl who doesn't deserve to get railroaded because it's easier to sack her than your son. I don't give a damn about your domestic situation or what you tell the rest of your staff. Frankly, it's been a long day. I'm tired, hungry, and as I just saved your ass, I think it's the least you can do. Wouldn't you agree?"

He nodded quickly.

"Good, so you'll call her in the morning. Tell her you're sorry, and you'd like her to come back. Then throw in a bonus, because you were such an asshole. Understand?" I hold his eyes as I give the instructions, making sure he understood I meant every word.

He nodded his head animatedly, then, with what was quite probably his last drop of courage, he asked, "Why do you even care?"

"I have a tender spot in my heart for lost causes and outcasts. I don't like seeing them taken advantage of, and I don't like the people that do it. Understand?" Venom dripped from my question, my intent to watch him squirm like a worm in bleach clear.

He nodded again before dropping his head to stare at his feet. He still had his shoes on.

"Right, well, now we've got that all worked out, I'll be on my way. But I'll be dropping by tomorrow for lunch. I trust no one will have a problem with that."

He looked back up at me and forced a big grin that, with the blood and swelling, would have given him a shot at the next Nightmare on Elm Street as Freddy himself. "Of course not. You're our most valued customer." Spoken like a true sycophant.

I matched the grin. "Good. I'll see myself out." I turned and took two steps but I suddenly realised in all this, there was something I still needed to ask and looked back. "Oh, by the way, what's that girl's name?"

He looked up, startled by such a strange question, given the circumstances. I couldn't blame him for that. Going through all this trouble when I didn't even know her name. I must have gone soft in the head.

He thought for a second, then said, a little uncertain, "Jane, Jane... err Porter."

Well, fuck me... what were the odds?

Chapter Five

I woke a little before dawn when the land was hazy with mist and the grey light of a shrouded setting moon. Dressing quickly in just a pair of tracksuit bottoms before downing a glass of orange juice, I set about my morning exercise. Quick but intensive, I took a five-mile run through the woods surrounding the property.

I'd always loved to run. There was something about running. It let me escape from everything, let me relax and fall into the moment. It was how I escaped my past and forgot the ghosts and demons haunting my shadows.

And it was why they had called me Tarzan.

I was always faster, more agile. The walking testimony that speed bettered brute strength and muscle. The streets of New York had been my jungle, and I'd mastered every part of them, from the stinking sewers to the highest rooftop. Nothing had been beyond my reach.

The forests of Washington were a very different sort of jungle, but the peace it brought was no less calming. And in the summer, it was a searingly beautiful scene. But summer was over, and in Autumn's harrowing march towards winter, there was just the grey and the silence. Mist stuck to my skin, making me feel cold and clammy as winds whispered through the trees, raising goosebumps across my naked torso.

Yet the cold served its purpose. It helped me keep my thoughts grounded in the now and off her.

Although all the drama yesterday had left me feeling dog tired, I'd barely been able to sleep a wink all night. My thoughts had just kept drifting back to the fiery little minx, Jane Porter.

And wondering what it would feel like to have her spread out beneath me.

The idea sent a delicious sizzle of heat rushing down to the base of my spine that I wasn't in too much of a hurry to force down.

It was a ridiculous thought. Of course it was.

I had no business even considering pursuing her, especially after the trouble I'd got her into yesterday. Even if it was indirect.

I was bad for her. I knew it, and she knew it. She knew it with that sixth sense all women possessed, and that drew them to only the most dangerous alpha males.

If experience had taught me anything, it's that there was no place for love or attachment in my life. The risks were too great. For them and for me. If someone got too close, they became a weapon to be used against you. A hostage to be grabbed and tortured, a potential target to be slain as a warning or a punishment. And even if they weren't the ones to go missing, there was the inevitable likelihood I wouldn't come home one day. That they'd be left waiting, dreading every ring of the phone would be that call from the hospital or the morgue. All the while scared that call might never come because they couldn't find my pale, bloated corpse in the river.

Or worse still, that my past would catch up to me. That one night there would be men at our door with duct tape, a do-it-yourself arson kit, and the message 'Alexi sends his regards.'

Fuck that, it was just too dangerous anyway you cut it. Only a true psychopath could ever invite someone into that sort of danger.

Except that didn't stop me from noticing how right she was for me. Just my type, in fact. A tiny little thing, all curves and legs, with a head of lush dark hair and a feisty little hell cat spirit. Like a leopardess in a cage.

If only I had the time to spare to pursue her. One day down on my five-day deadline, and all I had to show for my efforts was collateral and a promise. And that was the straightforward part of the job.

It was today things were liable to get complicated, and that was before getting to the matter of debt settlement. One slip up, and everything would spiral out of control into a serious drama.

Here was the part I needed to keep my head in the game. Where it belonged, instead of pining after Jane Porter's great ass and imagining what would surely be the fuck of the century.

The sun was up when the route led back to the barn. There were still clouds, but the grey light had turned a royal blue even as winter's bite kept gnawing at my ass. Going straight up the stairs to my living quarters, I made straight for the shower, dropping the joggers as I went.

The water was already scalding when it washed over me, like a rush of fire crashing across my face and down my back, cleansing me of the sweat and muck and chasing all my demons down the drain. It was as delicious as that first plunge into a hot bath and I stayed there under the spray, with head bowed and arms braced against the tiled wall. Quickly, the sting of burning needles dissolved into a deep, throbbing heat. It soothed all the aches from my run and all the lingering reminders from yesterday that I wasn't *that* man anymore.

The truth hurt, as they say, and usually it wasn't just a metaphor.

As the seconds turned into minutes, a curtain of steam rose around me. However, no matter how long I stayed there, I knew the water would never shake that one lingering thought from my mind. Just as I was certain it would never settle the very prominent stiffness standing rampant between my legs. Which just so happened to be growing increasingly uncomfortable as my thoughts drifted back to Jane Porter, and would make my task for today exceptionally difficult.

Fortunately, there was a sure-fire solution to both problems.

One of my hands was already halfway there when I made the conscious decision, my fingers closing around my length. Already hard, they could barely meet in the middle.

Fuck, what's wrong with me?

There wasn't any build up. Already wet from the shower, the first stroke had my head rolling back with a ragged moan. Christ, my dick felt like it was about to burst. What the hell had that little minx done to me?

As my hand pumped along my length, images of Jane Porter flooded my brain.

Bent over, hands flat against the wall, her head thrown back and a stream of soft wanton sounds flowed like music to my ears as I fucked her. Her lush ripe butt presented, her greedy cunt swallowing every inch as I went balls deep, wrapping around me, milking me, trying to wring the orgasm out of...

Fuck, I wanted her.

I wanted to find out what her pussy tasted like and how quickly I could make her cum. I wanted that smart mouth of hers on my cock, wanted to watch her going down on me for all she was worth. I wanted her under me, begging for me. To feel her clawing my back and hear her begging me to fuck her, take her, and know she was *mine...*

"Err... Fuck!" I grunted. Dark spots flashed before my eyes as that one thought triggered a release so intense it was almost painful. My breath came shallow and ragged as the waves crashed over me full force, and great shots of my seed splashed across the tiles. Only when the pulsing sensation down at the base of my spine had dissolved into a low throbbing did I dare risk moving.

My legs shook a little, but by some miracle I didn't fall flat on my arse. So, with my lust stated and once again able to think straight, I shut off the shower and stepped out onto the mat. Wrapping one ready towel around my midriff, I patted myself down with the other as I moved through the bathroom to the kitchenette.

Breakfast was far and away from the fry up I'd been looking forward to last night. However, as most of the ingredients were probably still lounging around on the Walmart floor, beggars couldn't be choosers.

If nothing else, at least I had the tea.

So, finally able to think and with a brew on, I fished out Mr Ritter's list of names, and got ready for work.

After a trip to McDonalds for a Double Sausage & Egg McMuffin.

My third and final target was a serious cluster fuck in the making.

Alphonse Fungabera was definitely not any sort of local small fry.

Like me, his family had emigrated to the States when he was just a boy, only from Rhodesia, rather than the UK, where they had been cattle ranchers.

Then the bush war came, and the eventual fall of the white government saw 150,000 white landowners get *persuaded* to leave their homes. However, Alphonse's family had avoided the exodus. Instead, they had emigrated, or 'taken the gap' as they put it, after selling everything they owned to a foreign consortium, just before the conflict went completely tits up.

Rather than moving out to Texas and resuming the family cattle business, however, they instead went out west, and opened a Casino, The Lion's Den. And I meant a casino. One of the huge monster profit machines that sat on the strip with all the extras. Even bi-weekly Siegfried & Roy performances that included the white tiger act.

The Lion's Den had sat proudly amongst the top ten of Las Vegas casinos. Until competitors had bought the new management out after he'd lost a gambling licence for the state of Nevada.

They had shut the casino down and demolished it less than a month later.

That was the official story in the papers, but there was only so much you could fit into a local newspaper column. If you knew the way things worked on The Strip, you could infer quite a lot.

It wasn't a hard story to figure out. After his father had lost a fight with cancer, Alphonse had inherited everything. Flush with dreams of expanding the family business, he had engaged in a sortie of power grabs, and got torpedoed for it.

That was the way the mob worked in Vegas. They played hardball. You had to accept the status-quo or face the consequences. They didn't appreciate young upstarts.

So having lost his family business and run out of Las dodge Vegas, the poorer but hopefully wiser Alphonse had moved up to Washington state. An attractive location for any entrepreneur because lucrative tax breaks allowed for businesses that would help bolster the tourist industry. Of course, that didn't mean they would just give anyone a casino. Even after cashing in all of his assets, Alphonse had had to borrow more, then sought a loan of several hundred thousand from Mr Ritter.

I imagine this was the account that had his partners so on edge. More than a quarter of a million wasn't cricket, even if they were both played with a hard ball. If I hadn't been working for a percentage, I might have even refused the job. You didn't just walk up and ask him to hand over the cash, then threaten to burn down his business if he refused. That only led to a back room with a big skinhead called Dusty who would be keen to give your knees an etiquette lesson. No, there would be banks and lawyers and middlemen to negotiate around.

And that was if you actually got to see the mark in the first place.

Judging by the pictures of The Lion's Den in the Vegas Reporter the day of its demolition, The Watering Hole was a major step down. More of a building block than high rise casino, it was a three-story rectangle of uniform lime-washed white blocks and blacked-out windows. Anywhere else in America, it would have passed for one of the official government buildings downtown. In this place, surrounded by natural beauty and the backdrop of the Olympic National Park just off route 101, it just looked bloody awful.

And the road leading up to it wasn't much cop either.

Like all modern sports cars, the sleek, lightweight design of the 911 had been designed for and tested on the Nurburgring. Off the smooth tarmac of the highway, it handled the gravel track with all the poise and comfort of a rhinoceros. It was almost a relief to swing the thing down the ramp into the underground parking.

Unsurprisingly, there were plenty of spots.

This wasn't Vegas or Monte Carlo. In the middle of Washington State, only the most conscript of professional gamblers played the tables after breakfast.

That thought gave me pause and for a moment, I wondered if the Watering Hole would have a breakfast buffet. I even teased myself with the idea of looking for it, but then thought better of it.

Cluster fucks in the making weren't the time to be lagging on a full belly. When the shit hit the fan, the contents were likely to end up all over your shoes. Better to be hungry and quick.

Besides, if all went well, in a few hours I'd be enjoying lunch in the Beached Whale and admiring Jane Porter's fine backside.

I swung the 911 into the bay nearest the elevator. There were two. This one was obviously for the punters. The other was an express elevator at the other end of the garage. There was a 'Staff Only' sign next to it and a small cluster of cars gathered around. Making a mental note to keep an eye out for where that came out, I killed the engine and climbed out. I left the NR-40 stashed away in the door pocket. This might not be Vegas, but Casinos the world over had long since learned security was anything but a dirty word. They did not look kindly on anyone trying to sneak in weapons. If they caught me, they'd consider me a thief and take me out back to meet Dusty the Skinhead. They would permit only licenced bodyguards to carry a piece inside, and then only for the most exclusive of guests. No one less than Prince William or Kim Kardashian. Even then, William would have to bring the wife along to make the cut.

So, I was walking into a cluster fuck in the making, armed just with my wits and winning personality. God help me.

It was a small elevator, scarcely big enough to hold four men, but it was fast and only took a few seconds to carry me up to the floor above. The control panel suggested it could also go up to the floors above, but there was a panel of numbered keys beneath it. My guess was you'd need a security key to reach at least one of those. I made a mental note to watch out for any staff punching in codes, then the doors opened with a chime and I walked into Las Vegas. Not the heart of the Strip, mind. The ceiling wasn't high enough for that, but definitely Vegas, or maybe Atlantic City. Long rows of slot machines lined either side of a plush red runner up to three rings of game tables in the centre of the room. Everything but an Elvis Presley impressionist singing *Viva Las Vegas*.

Oh, and punters.

The place was near dead. There were scarcely a dozen people not in the crisp white shirt and monogrammed waistcoat uniforms and all of them wore that desperate, haggard look. The look of the winners who had made that one bet too many. Losers that just didn't know when to call it a day.

I'd fit right in.

Keeping my head down, I walked right in, passed the empty coat check booth, down the red carpet and past the long lines of slot machines towards the tables. As I went, I spotted a corner that served as a bar with a scattering of tall circular tables and stools around it. Two more gamblers were there, nursing their woes and expecting to find all the answers to their troubles at the bottom of a glass. There was an elevator door nearby, but that was in the wrong place to connect to the staff's garage entrance. To the bar's other side, a little way down, there was a plain, reinforced door. Though unmarked, it had a simple key code and card reader where there should have been a handle. The security station.

The discovery got the wheels in my head turning.

So, when I got to the tables, I veered right, and went straight to the bar.

The bartender, a dour-faced man wearing the uniform's monogrammed waistcoat, though his shirt was black, scarcely raised an eyebrow at my order for water. When he put my order down on the bar, though, I swear I denoted a snort of something derogatory when I handed him a crisp fifty-dollar note in return.

There were even more mutterings when he handed me my change, but I didn't bother to count it. Just took my glass and moved down the bar to take the stool between the two other patrons. Lost in their drink, they only looked up when my change clinked down on the bar. The bartender had taken his revenge on me by giving it to me in the smallest possible denominations. Putting the water down, I busied myself with sorting the notes and coins, piling them up into respective piles, notes and then coins, one on top of the other.

I left them there. Pulling out my phone, I took a swig of my water and made a show of browsing through the notifications for a few minutes before putting it back. Then, getting up with my water, I casually walked away, leaving my change behind. I went right this time, towards the security door. Except now there was a step, and I stumbled like a drunkard, spilling half my glass across the floor. No one noticed, however, because at that very moment-

"Hey let go you bastard!" an angry voice shouted.

Another slurred back, "No it's mine, give it 'ere."

"It's mine!"

"Fuck off!"

The shouts and curses continued in a diatribe, but I didn't need to look back to know what had happened. The two at the bar were fighting for my 'forgotten' change, just like I'd planned. In those few piles of silver dollars, the men saw their salvation. A chance sent by the almighty for them to win their fortune. They would fight like devils for those few coins and notes.

Except they weren't devils. So when the security door opened, it should only have been a matter of time before the fracas calmed down. Which was why I'd taken my clumsy tumble. Instead, as a pair of gorillas in the casino uniform came running at full speed towards the commotion, their feet skidded out from beneath them. They went down hard in a heap on the floor. That would hopefully buy me all the time I needed.

In their haste to settle the disturbance in the bar, the security men had not stayed to make sure the door to their command centre shut securely. They'd just bolted, forgetting their drills in their rush to get to the scene. As they hurried out, I slipped around and inside, never a moment to spare, before the door slammed shut behind me.

Inside, the security room was little better than a closet. A walk-in closet that was barely ten feet by ten, including computing and storage space. There was a PC atop a desk in front of a bank of old-style monitors that made up one wall. A kitchenette sat opposite that, leaving just enough room in between for a locked metal gun cabinet with a live ammo sticker across the front.

I plonked myself down in one of the swivel chairs in front of the desk, pulled myself in while setting the remains of my water down, and got to work. Whichever one of the security team had been on monitoring duty hadn't been in too much of a hurry, so hadn't forgotten to put the system to sleep. When I fired it up again, a lock screen informed me I would need a login and password to proceed. Now why does that never happen in the movies?

Unperturbed, I took out my phone and a universal charger lead from my jacket pocket. Slotting the appropriate head into the phone's charging port, I plugged the other into the computer's USB port before scrolling my phone's apps menu. On the second page, there was an icon of a carton weasel done up like James Bond. The caption beneath read 'Sniffer'. Tapping it, my phone screen went black and a progress bar materialised. The weasel, still in his DIY Bond get up, snuck into the corner of the screen. He pulled a filing cabinet out of his pocket and began sniffing through the contents of a draw. On the computer screen, the log-in info and password appeared as the progress bar circled through, as if by magic. I was in.

Down on my phone screen, Weasel Bond gave me the thumbs up as I unlocked the computer, then another box popped up, again asking me if I wished to proceed. I confirmed with another tap, and the progress bar reappeared, only this time, as the weasel ferreted in the cabinet, long lines of code started scrolling down. That was exactly what I'd wanted to see. The list of all the files the Sniffer was copying to my predesignated cloud storage space via a VPN.

The only question now was, would it finish the job before my distraction got sorted out?

Fortunately, a quick glance across the monitors could tell me much of what I needed to know. The camera watching the bar showed the security men had gathered themselves up and were grappling with the drunkards and trying to manhandle them towards the door. Considering the difference in sizes, the offenders were putting up a better fight than anyone would have expected. Hard luck for the gorillas. They could call in backup to overpower the drunkards during the busy hours, but this was the graveyard shift. They were on their own.

Or perhaps the pair just weren't very good at their jobs.

Either way was good news for me. I guessed I had maybe five minutes before they came staggering back in here and found me playing with their computer.

My phone produced a squawking sound that rather reminded me of Woody the Woodpecker's laugh, only after he'd taken a kick to the balls, announcing the transfer was complete. Sure enough, a quick check showed James Weasel dancing a foxtrot with an imaginary partner in celebration. The designer clearly spent too much time watching cartoons. Shutting the app down before he started showboating for good measure, I disconnected the cable from the PC, then shoved both it and my phone back into my pocket.

After putting the computer back to sleep, I picked up my glass and poured the contents down the back of the PC.

This wasn't mindless destruction. Like its human likeness, the sniffer wasn't a subtle program. Its work was quick but messy, it left evidence of its presence. Evidence that wouldn't be hard to spot if someone even a bit tech savvy looked. Then it would only be a matter of time before they put two and two together. They'd spot my face, notice what I was doing, determine I had hacked their system, and then they'd be on the lookout for me. And the next time I stepped foot on the premises, they'd be on me.

Now, the moment they fired the system up, it would short circuit, wiping out all evidence of the sniffer and any reason to suspect I was anything but another punter. There would be questions about how the water got there in the first place, but when the security men couldn't answer, it would just get chopped up to human error. An incompetent staff member is always a more believable explanation than sabotage.

Glass in hand, I exited the security room without a backward glass, veering left and along the wall and around the slots, back towards the lifts. The trick when leaving the scene was not to draw any attention to yourself. It was easy enough, just move calmly with eyes front and head high, like you owned the place. Whatever you do, don't run. That was the most important part of an escape. Never run. Not until you needed to, anyway.

Over by the bar, things were settling down. The security men had their charges under control and were half escorting, half carrying them towards the exit. Pausing next to a line of slots, I gave the scene a curious glance while casually placing the glass down on the nearest machine. Then I turned on my heel and continued towards the elevator like nothing had happened.

Five minutes later, I was in the Porsche and away. I'd got what I came for and I'd check it over back at the barn. Until then, I was in the mood for a burger.

Chapter Six

Mikhail Kuznetsov hated America.

He hated everything about this cursed place.

He detested the small-minded, liberal society.

The weakness and greed of its government, the arrogance and ignorance of its people. He loathed it all.

Even the sheer hypocrisy of it all grated on him. A land built on conquest and bloodshed that claimed to champion the cause of justice, liberty and diplomacy while bullying the world with a policy of threats of military and economic reprisals.

How such a place still existed after 300 years baffled him and he hated it. Every bit of it.

He was a son of the Soviet Union.

His father had been a Narkom, a People's Commissar for the District Minister, his mother a receptionist for the Council of Ministers. They had raised him to be a son of the state. That state might be dead, but the Communist fires still burned in his heart. It made him who he was and had given him the dedication and loyalty to put his Bratva first, before any worldly wants and lusts of the flesh, before the duty he owed to a wife and family. He had devoted himself to his brotherhood and his Pakhan.

He didn't belong in this hotbed of capitalism, but his Pakhan had given him the order, and like any good soviet, he obeyed.

But what he hated most about this fragmented MTV rap-video culture was how it had corrupted and indoctrinated even the soldiers of their Bratva. Soldiers like Rory Novikov, or *Roy*, as he now called himself.

"Mikhail, what are we gonna do?"

The impotent worm. He even dared to address him by his given name. He didn't even speak to him with respect or call him Brigadier anymore. Ignoring the question, Mikhail broke out two ibuprofens from the pack in his desk drawer and washed them down with a swig of People's Pride vodka.

It burned like fire all the way down. That was what he liked about it. It was genuine Soviet vodka, a brew first concocted by the soldiers of the red army to help keep out the cold while they defended the motherland from the Nazis. Now, it was just about impossible to buy anywhere in the Americas or Western Europe. He imported a dozen crates every month from the only distillery left in mother Russia still manufacturing it. Its cost was outrageous, but all loyal sons of the state had to do their part.

Of course, everything burned after his impromptu lynching the previous evening. A fact that wasn't doing anything to improve his disposition to the man opposite him.

"Mikhail!" Rory snapped with such energy that Mikhail couldn't help glancing back up at the younger man. Amidst the old-world opulence of the Avtoritet's office, a man's space of hard wood and rich dark colours, he looked like a clown. A posing hard man in combat pants and a too tight t-shirt that showed off the cut of his muscles, desperate to disguise the fact he'd got his ass kicked twice the previous day and had spent much of the night heavily sedated while the best dentist in Seattle worked to save his teeth.

The soldiers of his unit, who'd been with him at the bar and were lounging around his office like it was their own personal club, were little better. If this was the future of the Bratva, Mikhail wept for his brotherhood and how far they'd fallen.

"What are we going to do?" Rory asked, in Russian this time. Perhaps he meant to emphasise the seriousness of the question, but his atrocious American born accent made it sound more like a bad Ukrainian comic.

Mikhail just stared back blankly. "About?"

"That fucking bitch at the bar," Rory snapped again, his temper flaring, and with it, he slipped back into English. "What will you do about him?"

The older man sighed mournfully. Rude, thick-headed, and just a downright bloody fool. Ivan would turn in his grave if he knew what his son had become.

Ivan had been Mikhail's brother in their Bratva. As boys, they had fought, side by side, in the streets of Moscow. As men, they'd come to America with their Pakhan. Together they had fought their way across the new world, annihilating or assimilating all the other factions of the Bratva, and given Alexi the greatest kingdom the world had ever seen. An empire stretching from east to west, the likes of which Hitler,

Napoleon, and even Stalin himself could only ever dream of. Mikhail had stood best man at his Ivan's wedding, and helped carry him to his grave, brother's side by side to the end.

He'd tried to watch over his brother's son, to guide him as a Dutch Uncle should, but the lad had been Americanised all the same. Now it was only the love he held for this boy's father that kept Mikhail from making an example of him right there.

Anyone else would be long dead and rotting at the bottom of the straits

Thinking of his old friend, Mikhail touched a hand to his Saint Vasily Medal and tried to remember the boy he'd raised. "Haven't you had your ass kicked enough for one day?" He said calmly, easing back into the big leather chair, knowing he needed to keep his control despite the cold worms that had wriggled their way into his guts through the night. "You just concentrate on your part. Leave the Englishman to me. He will be dealt with. I've already called New York."

He deliberately took his time with the words. Emphasising the last part with a finality that brokered no argument.

A sudden hush descended as all eyes in the office rounded on their Brigadier. Even Rory seemed to forget himself, momentarily humbled by the implication of the statement. "You called Alexi?"

Mikhail nodded. If it had been for any other reason, Mikhail would've congratulated himself, maybe even allowed himself a moment to dream there was some hope for him.

However, this was not the day.

That call had doomed him as much as any of the fools scattered around him. Still, what choice did he have? Ten soldiers assaulted or near enough, including himself, in a day, by one man. Whatever else he might be, that Englishman was a threat. An insect compared to the Bratva perhaps, but a dangerous insect all the same. One that needed to be squashed quickly. He'd be lucky to come out of this with his command. That being said, if Alexi had learned of it later that Mikhail had tried to cover up this shit storm, it would be he who would be made an example of.

Better to be a good soldier and take responsibility for this fuck up, then get caught trying to cover it up. The cemeteries of the Gulags were full of men who had made that mistake once.

"What did he say?" Rory pressed after a drawn out silence, a noticeable tremor in his voice. Mikhail couldn't blame him for that. Alexi wasn't known for his compassion. Whatever the story, the outcome would be the same. They had made his Bratva look weak. He would make up his own mind about who was to blame and how to deal with them.

Both their heads were as likely as not for the noose.

"The Pakhan-"

"Your Pakhan sent me."

All eyes in the room looked up to see a body standing just inside the office. No one had heard him enter.

He was not a tall man, nor especially large, but he was broad across the shoulders and had a powerful frame that filled out his three-piece suit so perfectly it could only be tailored. A man of means then, but his face was hard and craggy with none of the softness of someone born to money. So he'd made his money working with his hands.

The sight of him sent a sudden shiver of fear through Mikhail. There was something about the way the man stood. Confident, completely at ease but also alert, ready to spring at the slightest provocation, and something else. Something in the way his intense, baleful blue eyes stared out from their sunken sockets that suggested he was capable of terrible things. It was the aura of a predator, a trained killer. And he immediately felt the noose tightening around his neck. This was not a man to fuck with.

Rory was not so cautious and lurched up from his seat, full of fire and bravado in front of this man. "Who the fuck are you?"

The man ignored the question. Instead, he advanced, crossing the office and up the short flight of steps to Mikhail's suite. His predatory eyes fixed on the Avtoritet seated behind his desk. "I understand you have a problem, Brigadier."

His accent was Chechen.

Shit.

"Yes," Mikhail nodded, and thought of the Makarov pistol in the desk drawer. Would he have time to go for it if things went bad? With a distraction, maybe. Unfortunately, the men under his command were not so obliging. Perhaps the whipping the previous day had taught them the value of caution because, as the Chechen approached, they stepped back, fanning out to encircle, or just watch.

All except Rory, who stepped directly in his path. "Woah, where're you going?" he barked, putting a hand on his shoulder to halt the Chechen in his tracks. "I asked just who the fuck you are? Don't make me ask you again."

For a long moment, the man said nothing. Then he dragged his eyes away from Mikhail to the hand on his shoulder, then up at Rory. "Nemesis," he said, his tone even and somehow more threatening than if he had bellowed it in a war cry. "You know what that word means, don't you, boy? A righteous infliction of retribution manifested by an appropriate agent." The threat was plain as the Chechen held Rory's gaze.

Mikhail saw his chance and was just about to move for the desk drawer when Rory dropped his hand and stepped back.

The Chechen didn't acknowledge the victory. Instead, he just turned back to Mikhail and calmly took the seat Rory had vacated, as tranquil as if nothing had happened. Steepling his fingers, he said, "You need to keep a tighter leash on your dogs, Brigadier, before they get put down. Now, what's this problem of yours?"

The Beached Whale was as busy as I had ever seen it. There were two guys at the bar. A man and woman sitting at a table by the window, and another three guys sitting around a booth talking amongst themselves. No one looked up as I walked in and, blessedly, there wasn't a single Russian voice in the place.

Mike was back behind the bar, but this time, he refused to acknowledge me as I walked in. He just kept his head down as he poured the next round. Probably the best thing, really. I hadn't forgotten what he'd said yesterday about what had happened. I'd make a point of having a little talk with him later, but for now, I just wanted my burger.

"Oh no, here comes trouble," a familiar voice called as Debra stepped into view. However, there was no notepad or tray with a burger and chips in sight. That wasn't good. Nor did she call me Sugar Pie. That definitely wasn't good news.

"Hey Debra," I said, giving her my best winning smile as I sat down at my customary table, trying to play it cool. I had to give the cleaners credit, two fights in one day and it still looked just like it had before the kickoff.

"Now don't you give me any of that sexy English hotness, mister charming," she growled, coming to stand over me with her hands on her hips. "Ya know, you caused a lot of trouble around here. That poor girl lost her job over that fight." Though her anger seemed to be directed at me, as she said that, I could have sworn she shot the barman a dirty sideways glance. Guess she'd heard about him telling tales, too. Only, she shouldn't give him both barrels, so instead I was the one she was going to let out all her frustrations on. Lucky me.

"Yeah, I heard," I said, trying to both look ashamed and play innocent as the group at the other table started glancing our way. No point giving the regulars any more to gossip about. "So, I popped by last night to have a little chat with the boss, straighten it all out. She should be all good and in for her next shift."

"Well, you might have straightened it out with Mr Gates, but as I'm covering that shift, guess you didn't square it with her," She retorted in a matter-of-fact fashion, like she was telling her kids the hard truths of life. "She came in this morning, told him to forget it, then walked right back out again."

"Bloody hell!" I sighed, more exasperated than pissed off. Bloody women, never satisfied. Do them a favour and it's still not good enough. "Alright, when is he next in? I'll have another word. Find out just what's going on."

"You can talk to him right now. He's out back. I'll go get him if you-hey!" I don't wait for her to finish before I'm up out of my chair. All eyes spun in my direction, but now I didn't care and just stormed across the bar, past the kitchen window, through the doors to the games room and down a side passage marked staff only. Debra was hot on my heels. "Hey, you can't go back here."

She sounded flustered, no longer angry, probably more than a little nervous. "I'll only be a minute."

"You can't!" She gasped, panting a bit with the strain of keeping up with my longer strides. "Please, don't make me call Brian, our fry cook. You remember him, right?"

Yeah, I remembered him alright, and his knife, but it was too late. Spotting the door with the 'Manager' legend stamped across a brass plaque, I walked up and shouldered through, conveniently forgetting to knock. "Ned!"

Sat behind an unnecessarily large desk piled high with papers and books, Ned Gates looked no more impressive than he had on his back. His head snapped up at the interruption before his eyes went as wide as saucers. That must have hurt. The bruising around his face had matured into an ugly purple hue. No wonder he'd decided to do the accounts. One look at that face would convert even the most ardent alcoholic to sobriety.

Before either of us could say anything, Debra stepped around me, blocking my way, all tears and apologies, probably terrified she was about to get the boot too. "I'm sorry, Mr Ned, he wouldn't listen."

Poor love, she really didn't need this.

To his credit, Ned just forced a polite smile and raised a hand to calm her down. "That's alright Deb, I'm sure it couldn't be helped. You get back to the bar. I'll handle this."

She didn't look all that convinced to me and I doubt my best reassuring smile did much to console her. However, when Ned gave her the nod and a dismissing wave, she backed out of the office. Only when the door shut behind her did all the smiles drop.

"What the hell do you want now?" Ned asked, obviously desperate to get the first hit and salvage some of his dignity.

Luckily for him, I was willing to ignore his attitude, to a point. "I told you to give the girl her job back."

"I did. She didn't want it."

"Why?" I asked, walking across the small space to stand over him and his desk with my arms folded. It was a short walk. The room was hardly big enough to swing a cat in and had been filled with filing cabinets and dust-caked boxes of Beached Whale branded merchandise. It had a gorgeous sea view, though. Behind the desk, the huge panel windows looked out across the Salish sea. On a cloudless summer day, I bet Ned could see all the way across to Vancouver Island. Maybe that was why he had picked this glorified coat room as his office.

Ned swallowed, obviously trying to look unworried but failing miserably. "Why what?"

"Why didn't she want it? Yesterday she said she needed it," I pressed, leaning down and bringing our faces close enough for me to inhale his atrocious aftershave.

And see the sweat forming on Ned's forehead.

"How am I supposed to know? What am I, a psychic hotline?"

Narrowing my eyes, I keep my voice low but stare at him hard as I ask, "What did you say when she came in?"

"Good morning, I think," he said, his bruises turning ever deeper, more livid shades. "She took one look at me, screamed something, then threw off her apron and ran out."

I arched my brow. "That's all?"

"Yeah, that's all," He half shrieked, his eyes going wide again as he edged back in his chair to put a bit of distance between us. "Listen, I did what you asked. I called her up, apologised, gave her the job back, and even offered a raise. It's not my fault if she changed her mind. What more do you want from me?"

Satisfied, I straightened up and smiled jovially down at him. "I want her address."

Somehow, his eyes got even wider. "What? I can't tell you that."

"Her address, where she lives. Tell me and you'll never hear from me again."

"But… I can't. It's illegal to give out employees' personal details." He looked around desperately, as if trying to find a solution to this fresh problem written on the walls. One thing was sure, he wouldn't find it out the window.

"She quit, remember."

Giving up his search, he turned back to me but couldn't meet my eyes. "It's still against the law to give out personal details."

At any other time, I could have admired his resolve, but right now, I needed her address. She had some explaining to do.

I swivelled my head around, looking around the office with exaggerated slowness. "Fine, don't give it to me. I'm sure it's around here somewhere. Maybe I'll just pop by tonight to take a look for it. Then who's to say where or how I got it-"

There was a loud knock on the door.

"Everything all right, Mr Gates?" A deep voice asked through the door and I remembered the fry cook with the big knife. Looks like Debra had followed through with her threat after all. Or had he heard Ned's balling? He was making enough noise for the entire bar to hear.

Together we glanced at the door, then back. When our eyes locked, he knew he had to make a choice.

It was crunch time. He could break the law or call in the cook and risk getting a whole lot more broken.

He made his choice.

"Yeah, all good, Brian," he replied, grabbing a pen and scribbling quickly across a notepad before tearing it off and shoving it my way. "Fine, there!"

"Thank you," I smiled, taking it and folding it into my pocket.

It was time I paid Miss Jane Porter a visit.

Chapter Seven

Downtown Port Angeles looked rather like uptown, midtown, and every other residential part of the city. A varied collection of single and two-storey timber fronted cottages with paved driveways and big front gardens. The whole place had the feel of a quaint little suburbia where everyone and their dog knew your name and your business.

In other words, what I'd call hell.

Fortunately, I wasn't here to admire the view. I wanted answers, and according to Ned's scribble, Miss Porter lived at 13 King's Way. The name meant nothing to me but courtesy of my phone's Maps App, it didn't take long to navigate the warren and turn the Porsha off West 10 Street. For all the grandeur of its name, King's Way proved to be just another quiet little street ending in a cul-de-sac with about half a dozen single storey cottages around it.

Number 13 was the first on the left. A single storey cottage painted baby blue, with a wraparound porch, likewise painted cedar red, and a 2004 Ford Explorer Sport Trac 4x4 on the drive.

I parked the Porsche up behind the pickup, killed the engine, climbed out and marched up to the house, not caring if she was alone or if someone was in there with her. If I was lucky, maybe she had a boyfriend over and I could work out some of this frustration on his face.

Until then, her door would do. I knocked three times, banging my fist against the wood hard enough to make it rattle in the frame. Then I waited.

Damn her, I got her that fucking job back, so what was her problem? What was she playing at?

I knew I needed to breathe. I was pissed off and had to calm down, but I wasn't in the mood for all that crap right now.

"Coming!" Jane's voice called from inside.

Footsteps approached from the other side of the door. A chain rattled. Then the door opened and Jane Porter stood there in a pair of tight little white shorts and a blue and red checked shirt, her hair tumbling down her back in a wash of raven waves and smiling as she read something on her phone. "Mrs Wilde, I'm afraid this isn't really a great time, 'cause I just lost my job and I- you!" Her smile dropped when she looked up and saw me standing in her doorway.

Praise where praise is due, Miss Jane Porter was not slow to react. No sooner did she see me than she was slamming the door in my face. It's not exactly an original move, though. Nor was it the first time someone had tried it. I shouldered my way through before she could shut it all the way. She almost went with it, skidding backward, but I caught her wrist and twisted her round, driving her back against the wall. The door swung closed behind us as I slapped a palm over her mouth to keep her from screaming and stepped in close enough to pin her there, caging her with my body.

I expected her to fight. To lash out and squirm, or kick, bite and scratch at anything she could reach with all that fiery spirit she'd shown when Roy and his mates had surrounded her. Instead, she just stood there, with her arms hanging at her side and eyes as large as dinner plates.

"Scream, and I'll gag you, understand?" I warned, keeping my voice low and level but looking dead into her eyes so she knew I meant it.

She nodded slowly. Or, at least, gave as much of a nod as she could with half of her face in my hand and nowhere to move. Still, I had to give her points for effort.

"Good," I said, forcing a little smile to soften my expression as I eased my hand back a little. "You know, you should really check who's at the door before you open it."

"Please…" she whispered, her voice shaky, clearly too unnerved for levity. "What… what do you, I mean, what are you doing here?"

"Why did you quit your job?"

"What?" She blinked, as if that was the last thing she'd been expecting.

"You heard. Why did you quit your job at the bar? Last night you said you needed it, so I got it back for you. Now I hear you've quit, and I want to know why."

My question seemed to steady her, however, and she visibly hardened under my interrogation. "Because of you, you asshole!" she spat back, suddenly all fire and venom. "Because of what you did."

"Me? What did I do?" It was my turn to play dumb. Admittedly, it helped that I didn't have a clue what she was going on about.

"Don't bother. I saw Ned's face! You beat him to a bloody pulp!" She accused, beating her hands on my chest. "Who the fuck do you think you are? You can't just go around beating people to get what you want! And why? To get me my job back after you fucked it all up! Do you think I'd accept anything from you after what you've done?"

Oh fuck!

That's what this was all about. The beating the Russians had given Ned. Of course she'd think that was my handiwork work, why wouldn't she? She hadn't known he'd had company when I arrived and sounds like she hadn't stuck around long enough to ask.

No wonder she's pissed off.

I backed away a step, giving her some space, raising my open-palmed hands in a universal show of innocence while trying to calm the fuck down. "Hey, hey, cool it, I didn't do that."

"Fuck off!"

"Really, Scout's honour, he was like that when I found him, and anyone at the bar will tell you I didn't do that to him."

She crossed her arms. "Oh yeah? How?"

"Because he looks too damn good." Probably not the best choice of words, but I couldn't help myself. Fine ass or not, her attitude was really grating on me.

Her eyes flashed dangerously, as cool and as sharp as ice. "Bullshit. Who else would do something like that?"

"Roy and his friends from yesterday, that's who," I snarled back through gritted teeth. "They came by to play a game of twenty questions with your boss, and they didn't like some of his answers. If I hadn't arrived when I did, chances are he'd be taking a trip into intensive care right about now, with you in the bed next to him, but don't worry, I took care of it. They're all sorted. If you don't believe me, go ask, then you'll see what it looks like when *I* give someone a slap."

She wasn't in a mood to accept my reassurances and pressed on relentlessly, stabbing a finger into my chest. "Nothing will ever be sorted so long as there are people like you in the world. Yeah, I know your sort. You walk around like you own the place. Like you can do and take whatever you want. Selling drugs and guns, turning honest people into junkies and whores desperate for their next fix! Men like you, *and Roy*, you're all the same. Animals! Nothing but dogs fighting over a bone, and you'll bite anyone that tries to stop you!"

Okay, this time she had gone too far.

This girl had been rude since the moment she first saw me. She'd accused me of beating up her boss- which I hadn't- and of getting her fired- okay, that I might have had a hand in, indirectly. Now she was calling me a dog and saying I was no better than Roy, a Russian thug that had threatened and abused her. A stinking, filthy Russian animal!

There was a time when she might have been almost right. The streets of New York City were dangerous places. No one lived on them and came out clean, and there were times I'd done things I wasn't proud of to survive. As a boy, the law of the jungle, that concrete Manhattan jungle, had ruled my life. Then, after Don DeCampo took me in, I had changed. Since the day Turk found me, I'd hurt men. I'd killed them and watched them die, but they were all a part of that dark criminal world, never real people. Never innocent. I'd never stolen from honest people, peddled drugs or made women whores.

And when he put that bullet in my head, I was reborn.

That bullet gave me a second chance, a new life.

A life out of that shadow world for good.

I didn't care what she'd seen me or anyone else do. That wasn't an excuse.

I wasn't a fucking animal.

It was time she learnt that.

Miss Jane Porter had been a very naughty girl.

And naughty girls get spanked.

"Is that so?" I didn't wait for an answer, just grabbed her arm and spun her around to push her against the wall. She gave a small squeak of surprise, then went silent as I cupped her nape. Then I was caging her again, and leaning down I said, "you know nothing about me."

"Yes, I do, you're… dangerous," she whispered, her voice shaky and eyes wide with animal panic.

"And you like it, don't you?" Catching her wrists, I raised them up over her head and pressed them hard to the wall. Securing them both with my left, I brought my right down.

"What? No! Of course no- Ahh!" She gasped as I gave her right cheek a smack that was a little less than gentle, but produced a very satisfying crack. "What the fuck?"

"It's not nice to lie." I left my hand there for a moment, enjoying the feel of her ass in my hands through the thin cotton of her shorts, so soft yet also firm and tight. Only when I was sure that the first sting had faded did I raise the hand again, only this time I brought it down on her left cheek.

"*Ow*! Wait! What are you doing?" She shot back, looking back at me, her eyes sparkling like diamonds.

I raised my hand to spank her again. "Teaching you a lesson."

"What?"-*smack*- "No!" She wriggled and twisted and tried to slip free of my hold on her wrists, but lacked both the strength and leverage to escape.

"I'm sick of your attitude. It's time I taught you a lesson in respect." I told her, yet even as I spanked her again, her struggles sent a delicious thrill through me and straight down to my stirring cock. Damn, this girl had some fire. Even when trapped and collared, forced into submission, she tried to resist, to fight. I liked it. Or maybe it was just the way her body kept rubbing against mine.

Either way, I held nothing back, and there was nothing Jane could do but endure it.

"You can't…" she protested as I spanked her again and again, each a little harder than the last. "Can't do this!"-*Smack*- "You bastard!"-*Smack*.- "I'll…"-*Smack*- "I'll call the cops"-*Smack*- "I'll do it, I swear-fuck!"

"Oh, will you now?" My hand was tingling from the repeated spanking, and I could actually feel the heat radiating through her shorts.

"Yes. Yes! I swear I fucking will. I'll do it, you fucking bastard!" Jane promised through gritted teeth. She spoke with such fire and venom. I could almost have believed the threat, but for all her fervour, I couldn't help noticing the flush that was spreading across her cheeks, nor the way she was biting down on her bottom lip.

I smiled knowingly to myself, then leant forward further to whisper in her ear. "Then ask me to stop. "

There are certain things you have to learn quickly to survive the Famiglia.

One of the most important lessons is to know the difference between a stuck up cow and a little princess in need of a good, hard fuck.

You had to learn it quick. Get it wrong, and some Caporegime might just lope off your balls for his prick teasing daughter's imaginary honour.

Jane Porter was definitely the latter.

The little minx was enjoying this. She just didn't want to admit it, most of all, to herself.

Then she opened her mouth, and for a single, long moment, I thought she would say it, but then she closed it again and looked away, refusing to meet my eyes.

"Go on," I pressed, and gave her ass another smack. She jumped at the contact, but still refused to speak. "All you have to do is say stop, and I will." I leant in closer. My voice was a low growl in her ear while I lay my spanking hand down on her abused buttocks. "That's what you want right, for me to stop and go?"

She gasped as I cupped her derriere, not so much squeezing as kneading the tender flesh through her shorts, massaging the pain away. It was a soft sound, almost too low to hear her mutter "No."

"What was that?" I goaded, applying a little more pressure with my hand, rubbing small circular motions so that my fingers brushed along the crack and down between her thighs. I knew it. She was wet!

"Please… don't stop," she moaned, loud and clear, her back curling and eyes shut tight in pleasure as I teased across her cleft through her soaked shorts.

It was music to my ears and turned my cock to steel.

I wasn't an animal, not anymore, but there was a time I had been a lion. And even dressed as mutton, when the lion rested amongst the sheep, he felt the need to hunt from time to time.

And when the lion's hungry, he eats.

Today, I would devour Miss Jane Porter.

"I thought not. Now, don't even think about moving." I tell her, releasing my grip on her wrists to place both hands on her shorts. She whimpered, but followed my instructions to the letter and stayed still as I hooked my thumbs under the hem of the garment, and whatever she was wearing beneath, and pushed them all the way down her long legs to the floor.

I was right. Her ass was amazing.

"Up," I barked, tapping the calf of her right leg so she'd understand what I wanted. She raised it obediently, and I kicked the garments aside before signalling for her to lower it again. As I came back up,

I trailed my hands along the inside of her legs, wanting and needing to touch her.

I had to admit, she had the softest skin, warm and as smooth as melted caramel.

"Is this what you want?" I did not hide my amusement, enjoying the way her whole body trembled as my fingers brushed over the inside of her knees and up her thighs, moving higher and higher-

"No!" Jane sobbed out, her voice soft, needy and unconvincing.

"Liar." I gave her bare ass a slap with my left that had a crack like a whip and left a noticeable handprint across her bronzed skin. My handprint. My mark. I'd branded her with my mark. She was mine.

And to prove it, I brushed a finger of my right across her folds, gathering up her cream and spreading it over her hood. Her clit was already swollen and begging me for attention, betraying how much her body was enjoying this. She moaned a low, throaty sound, but otherwise remained silent and bowed her head in contrition, accepting and needing more.

"Your cunts drenched, you naughty girl," I told her, coming back up to lean over her as I strummed her bundle of nerves before sliding the finger down into her slick warmth.

"Oh god... please... no... I... I can't..." Her voice was shaky and she couldn't quite form the words amidst the stream of husky moans that all went straight down to my cock as I explored her body.

"Shhh… It's okay to want this, love." Her walls fluttered around my fingers when I used the endearment, letting me know she liked it. Fuck, I loved how responsive she was. I circled the digit, feeling around her slickness before curling it. Her whole body jumped when I found her sweet spot, and I focused all my attention on that one spot. "You like it, don't you? Like it when I spank you, when I finger this naughty little pussy until you cum all over my hand."

"Yes!" she gasped as I slid a second finger into her warmth, pumping slow and deep to heighten her sensory overload and wishing it was my cock inside her.

Fuck, she was so warm and snug.

I can't take much more of this.

I needed to be inside her, feel her wrapping around me, hear her beg for more as I go balls deep. Needing to know I was driving her as mad as she had me. "You want this. Say it," I demanded.

"Yes… Yes!" The words came thick and fast as she lost herself in the feelings I was stirring inside her, her back bowing as I fucked her with my fingers.

"Say it, say you want it." She was getting close. I could feel it building, the tightness in her body, her muscles tensing as she pushed back into my hand, grinding herself on my fingers.

"Yes, yes, I want it, I want it- what, no! Don't stop!" She almost shrieked in panic, her tone suddenly shrill with need and desperation as I pulled my hand away.

"I told you not to move," I reprimanded, grinning inwardly as I gave her ass another slap with my left that made her gasp a delicious little hiss. Then I brought my right hand up so we could both see how wet and shiny she'd left my fingers and inhale the musky scent of her arousal. "What do you want?"

She stared at my fingers for a moment, stared at the blatant truth of her desire and need, the reality of what I had done to her, then she threw a look back at me. "You… you bastard." Her eyes were dark with lust, but she held my gaze defiantly, owning it. "I want your fucking cock. So just fuck me already!"

She didn't need to tell me twice.

It took all of three seconds for me to get my jeans open. Then, after pushing them halfway down my legs, I gripped her hips and thrust.

"Oh… oh my god!" she moaned, her eyes going wide, that sexy mouth dropping open in a long moan as I passed through her folds and slid into her cunt.

And fuck, she felt incredible. Slick and warm and so fucking snug. Her body wrapped around my cock like a silken glove, and I couldn't stop my hips from curling into her warmth.

"Fuck... you feel so good," I grunted, swept up in the moment, taken by the thrill of fucking this woman I hardly knew. Driven wild by the sheer eroticism of seeing her bent over, of watching my cock slide through her folds and come out dripping with her cream. It was so primal. Bestial and pure instinct. The animal instinct to take and claim what was mine.

Jane was right there with me, pushing back to meet me, her slurred breathless sobs and mews of pleasure every time I sunk a little deeper, spurring me on. Driving me to go harder, faster, until-

"Oh fuck! Too much... so deep..." she gasped as I dragged her back to meet me, burying my cock in her all the way to the root. I was almost afraid I'd gone too far, but no sooner had I paused to let her adjust than she was thrusting back against me, demanding more. "Oh-my-god, oh-my-god, yes, just like that, just like-oh fuck!"

"Is this what you want?" I asked, giving her ass another swat before reaching down to palm her mound. Her body shuddered at the contact and her pussy clenched, milking me as I rubbed her clit.

"Yes! Yes, this... this is exactly what I want... please... punish me... split that naughty pussy open... I deserve it... make me cum... make me cum all over your big fucking... oh!" she moaned out before throwing her head back, her voice fading away as the waves of her orgasm crashed over her.

I fucked her through it. Delighting in the way her eyes rolled back, and her fingers turned white as she clawed desperately at the wall for support. Savouring every moment as she rose higher and higher to the heavens, shaking so violently that if I hadn't been supporting her, her legs would have given way. All the while knowing I'd done this to her.

It was one of the sexiest sights I'd ever seen.

A view I knew I could never tire of.

A work of art I wanted to spend the rest of my life appreciating.

And as she reached her peak, I felt my release building, felt the sense of it erecting down near the base of my spine. Her every cry and plea for more pushed me closer and closer.

Yet it wasn't enough. I needed more. Needed to touch her, feel her, taste her.

I needed… her.

I didn't question the urge, just acted upon it.

Letting go of her hip, I cupped her face and dragged her head around to crush my mouth to hers. Her hands buried themselves in my hair, fisting and twisting and tugging me closer as my tongue found hers, and the raw hunger with which she returned the embrace pushed me over the edge.

I came inside her, raw and balls deep, and knew, whatever happened after, I'd regret nothing.

The only way to live a good life is to live by your emotions and know you're doing what's right for you, in that moment, with no regrets.

This woman, she was infuriating, combative and a downright pain in my arse, but I could already tell there was so much more to her. More than just her beauty. She was passionate and fearless, brave and tenacious, would challenge me, ground me, and just cut through all the bullshit. I wanted to see those sides of her.

"So… um, what's your name, anyway?" she asked when we finally broke apart. Not looking at me, she straightened her shirt, then bent down to pick up her discarded shorts.

I tried not to grin at the handprint that was still branded across her otherwise perfect bum.

"I'm John," I replied, shoving my still semi-hard cock back into my jeans and doing up the fastenings.

Pushing a stray wing of her raven hair out of her face, she looked back at me and smiled shyly. "Hi John… I'm Jane. Pleasure to make your acquaintance."

"The pleasure, I'm sure, is all mine." I offered my hand.

She blushed but took my hand. "If you say so."

And just like that, the tension was broken and I couldn't help smiling back at her. "Well, now we've got formal introductions over with. Why don't you go get yourself cleaned up, then I'll take you out for dinner, and we can discuss what sort of man you think I am."

What are the odds?

John and Jane.

Me Tarzan, you Jane.

Chapter Eight

"So, if I understand this situation of yours correctly, Brigadier," the Chechen said, his voice still so deadly, despite the contempt blazing in those baleful blue eyes. "Your men, assembled here, were drinking in a bar yesterday."

Standing around the desk, the men in question at least had the good sense to keep their heads down and their mouths shut. They had all kept silent during the refined retelling of the previous day's events, none keen to incur the Chechen's ire. All except Rory, who stood with his arms crossed and a sulky, petulant look that only seemed to enhance his bruising.

"Yes," Mikhail nodded, his mouth dry around the single syllable that could so easily sign his own death warrant.

"They took a liking to one of the serving girls, an *Eskimo whore*," The Chechen spat out the words, but it was hard to tell if it was because he disapproved of the derogatory terminology or the idea of the Bratva's soldiers fucking an indigenous girl. There was a reason the phrase 'political correctness' did not translate into Russian. "But when they approached her, she was rude and disrespectful, so they corrected her. That should have been the end of the matter, except one patron interfered and overpowered your five men single handed-"

"It wasn't single handed," Rory snarled, causing the stranger to look up.

"Oh? I misunderstood? There were others?"

But Rory did not answer, though the cords along his neck stood out like creeper vines.

"He-he had a pool cue," a voice spoke up from the gathered soldiers, just loud enough to be heard but not to determine the speaker

"Of course, that makes all the difference." Disdain coated the Chechen's words.

"And a pint glass," another mumbled through the bandages that hid the marks left by one such glass.

The Chechen turned back to Mikhail. "I stand corrected. One man overpowered your five soldiers with a stick and a piece of glass." His lips pressed into a tight, humorous line that made the Avtoritet want to drain the last of his vodka. "Then, once they recovered their wits, your men tucked tail and ran to report this offence to you, Brigadier. Whereupon you and your personal guard, along with the captain here," he gestured to Rory, "return to the bar to question the owner. What was it you expected to learn again?"

Mikhail swallowed and hoped against hope he sounded more confident than he felt. "I needed information."

"Well, we always need information."

"A name, or a bank account number, even a picture of his face," he pressed, suddenly defiant, needing to justify himself. "Anything to help me find the Englishman."

"And instead, he found you."

That one question was enough to deflate and humble Mikhail, and he sunk back into his seat with a shrug. The Chechen had humbugged him, and he knew it. "Yes."

"You tried to take him, but instead he laid all your men out, barehanded this time," the man pressed. "And even made you agree to peace."

"With a noose around my neck, yes." It was an insignificant point, but Mikhail thought it worth mentioning all the same. Men had done much worse on pain of hanging, and at least he hadn't pissed himself.

"I see." There was a note of finality to the Chechen's words this time, as if he had come to his decision. He laid his hands flat on the table. "Please, Brigadier, enlighten me. What the fuck is wrong with you? And your *soldiers*?" As he spat out the word, there could be no doubting his contempt this time.

Rory had had enough. His face red, he stepped forward and bellowed. "Nothing is wrong with us! That English bitch insulted the brotherhood. He needed to be made to pay!"

"Insulted the brotherhood or you?" The Chechen scoffed, and for the first time, his perfect mask appeared to crack with irritation at the interruption. However, he ignored it this time and kept his gaze hard on Mikhail. "Tell me Brigadier. Have you read Clive Cussler or Lee Child?"

"No, I can't say I have." What was he about to invite him to a book club? Did he look the type to debate Bridget Jones and Tom Clancy over a glass of wine, vol au vents and caviar?

"I thought not. Based on your background, I don't think they would interest you. They're pulp mostly, little good for anything but wiping your arse with. The feeble imaginings of mad, drunken capitalist swine. But beneath their propaganda, there is a warning. You see, all those stories start the same. With a nobody stumbling across the villain's plans. He knows nothing, but the villain insists on trying to liquidate him as a precaution. And when they fail, that nobody comes looking for answers and foils their plot. Yet if they had left him alone, they would have succeeded, you see?"

"I see." Mikhail didn't, but he didn't see any point in arguing. "A most amusing parallel."

"I didn't mean it to amuse you, Brigadier," the Chechen growled, a warning edge to his tone that demanded silence. "The Englishman, what is he? Nothing. He didn't know who he was fighting. It was a bar fight, nothing more. He did not disrespect or challenge the brotherhood because he was unaware he was against the Bratva. He just wanted to help a girl who was being harassed by drunken buffoons. Had your men identified themselves instead, before engaging in a pissing contest with a superior opponent, this all could have ended differently.

"Then in your stupidity you go to find him, and instead he finds you, again to help this woman. This Englishman is a fool, suffering from a *Sir Galahad* complex, perhaps, but a fool nonetheless. A fool with some skill, that is all. And I do not wish to see the Pakhan's entire Western hub come crashing down because we insisted on chasing after a man of no consequence. He did the Bratva no insult. He had cause for the fight that did not involve business, and what's more, he wants peace. So he will have his peace."

If this man spoke it, then it was as good as spoken from Alexi's own mouth. There would be no vendetta against the Englishman.

Mikhail sighed and nodded, knowing what was coming.

Rory looked at the men at the desk in incomprehension. "But he took down several of our men. He must answer for this."

"Yes, someone must," The Chechen agreed and stared hard at the Avtoritet. "And the responsibility lies with you…"

Time seemed to hold its breath and Mikhail felt like all the snakes in his guts were readying themselves to rush at once out of his arse.

"Rory Novikov."

Despite himself, Mikhail couldn't help letting out a sigh of relief.

A hushed silence fell around the office as the soldier tried to comprehend what had just passed. Rory's mouth gaped like a fish as he tried to make sense of what he was hearing. Then the colour drained from his face with comprehension and he let out a nervous laugh. "What? Me? You can't be serious."

"Yes, you," said the Chechen, rising out of the chair and turning to face him. The hard line of his mouth twisting to bare ivory fangs. "You were there in both instances. It was you that allowed your men to get drunk on duty. You who alerted your Brigadier to a non-existent threat, and it was you who turned this whole messy affair into such a shit show. That is, what is the expression, three strikes. You're out, Rory Novikov."

Rory glanced at Mikhail, unsure, his eyes downcast and pleading. The Chechen advanced on him. "Mikhail?"

However, his father's friend just shook his head, helpless to do anything but disobey *Roy* and the westernised fool he had become. "I'm sorry Rory."

In a man's life, conflicting loyalties will always be forged, tested and tried. Mikhail had loved Ivan as a brother, but he was dead and gone. And if it came to a question of where his loyalties lay, to his fallen brother or the brotherhood and his Pakhan, he knew on what side of the line he stood.

It was time. He couldn't protect the boy anymore. He was a man of the Bratva who had just fucked up once too often.

As if coming to the same conclusion, his soldiers slowly started backing away. Realising the truth, that for the first time in his life, he was alone, Rory slowly started backing away. "But you can't. I know people. I have friends. Alexi will have your head if you-"

But the Chechen didn't care about Rory's threats and brushed them aside. "The Pekan doesn't know you. You have no friends. Your Brigadier was your only protection, but he has abandoned you now. Your father's reputation won't save you *Roy*, he's dead and gone, a worthless pile of shit and bones, just like you-"

Rory plunged forward, bellowing at the top of his lungs, his fear replaced by blind fury at the insult of his father.

It was a murderous attack, yet as his fist came down, the Chechen made no move to evade. He just suddenly went still, as if frozen in fear. Then he pivoted slightly, stepping out of the line of fire while moving his hands up and around. His left coming up to defend, grabbing the other man's wrist and dragging it in closer to throw him off balance while simultaneously punching with his right, first a quick hard jab to the solar plexus that became a swift uppercut to the jaw.

Mikhail had never seen such speed, such violence.

That Englishman was fast, but this… this man was in a whole other league.

Yet the Chechen wasn't done. As his hands did their devastating work, his off leg drove up hard into the back of Rory's knee, taking the leg out so his body dropped. Then he was twisting, throwing him to the floor.

Rory tried to go with it. To hit the ground with a roll the way Mikhail had taught him, but the Chechen was already moving. He dropped with him, driving his knee down into the point between his shoulder blades, pinning him there on his front. As he did, he tugged the knot of his tie loose and away so that it came free in his hands.

Blind to the coming danger, Rory struggled and twisted desperately to free himself and with his body tight, it took only one simple move to drop the loop under the man's neck before a great tug had them suddenly to their feet. Too late Rory's hands came up to tug at the length of grey silk around his jugular, because the Chechen was again moving and he had no choice but to go with him as he turned and twisted, both hands swinging the tie and man both around. Momentum more than anything carried Rory over the suite's bannister when he hit the rail, sending him over the drop. Yet the Chechen held firm, his leg coming up to brace against the barrier and take the other man's weight as he hauled him up so his body hung suspended, the tips of his shoes dancing a jig.

A high pitched sound, half cough and half scream, was his only swan song.

Mikhail heard the strangled sounds, the desperate choking of his ward, but didn't look away. This was on him. This was his failure and his punishment. Roy, no, Rory had been his responsibility, and he'd failed him. It was his duty to watch him die, to remember his suffering, and let it fuel his quest for vengeance.

Vengeance against those that brought his friend's boy to this pathetic end.

Vengeance against the Chechen and the Englishman.

Then silence descended.

Around Mikhail, the soldiers who had watched Rory grow up, who fought and drank with him, watched him die without a word. None dared speak out or try to interfere, and only when he was sure Rory was dead did the Chechen lope the ends of the tie around the railing and knot it.

"Leave him until the meat stinks, then take pictures and hang them there in his place, then leave the space next to them free, large enough to hang another. A warning to all that forget the price of failing the brotherhood." Then he turned and sneered at Mikhail, the baleful violence blazing in his cold blue eyes as bright and hard as a diamond. As if he hadn't just killed a man with his bare hands. "You will retain your command, but you will act under my direct supervision. Is that in any way unclear?"

Mikhail swallowed down the curse that was rising in his throat. "No."

"Good."

The statement hung in the air, yet there was more to it and Mikhail felt a sense of foreboding roll down his spine, like a black lake for the snakes that still roiled in his belly to slither into. He couldn't help pressing.

"That's this matter dealt with, then?"

"No, not quite. This bar. What is its name?"

"The Beached Whale."

"*Vybroshennyy na bereg kit.*" He nodded. "So long as it stands, the memory will endure. Remove the bar, and the incidents will be forgotten. Like they never occurred. I will take care of that tonight. You will find me a list of relevant persons we have in our pocket. Understood?"

Mikhail's head swam with all the things that he could mean and the ramifications to their business. "I understand."

He nodded. "Don't fail your Pakhan again, *Brigadier.*" With that final, unspoken threat, he turned on his heel and moved down the steps. Again, no one interfered or dared get in his way.

Mikhail watched him go, but as the Chechen neared the door to the office, he found his eyes drifting back to the railing. He stared at the knotted tie and couldn't stop himself.

"What's your name?" he called, then by way of explanation added, "for his mother."

The Chechen froze at that, dropped his hand and turned back to face the Avtoritet. From where he stood, he'd seen it all. He'd glimpsed the stunned soldiers on the suite, the commander at his desk, and the body hanging from the bannister, and smiled. He understood the request. A mother had the right to know the name of her son's executioner. Vengeance ran as thick as vodka in their blood. He had made an enemy the moment he slew Rory. It would probably just be another drop in the ocean, but she had the right to know.

His eyes moved from Rory's blue and swollen face to Mikhail, and his smile was suddenly a wolf's grin.

"Kleyton."

This is not the end.
John and Jane will return.

Now please enjoy this little sneak preview of

Reaper

In any situation you have a moment to turn everything around. One chance to save yourself before the choice is taken out of your hands.

Instead I did in fact, royally drop a bollock.

I just stared dumbly, mouth open like a fish as I looked from Anthony to Lucca, then back again. Their dull, unmoved looks and rather sadistic twists to the mouth telling me I better bloody believe this was happening.

While their steady grip and fingers on their triggers warmed me, I'd have been dead if I made any wrong move.

"Please don't fight, brother." Turk's voice was sombre, but resolute.

Slowly, my gaze swivelled back to him.

I bet the look on my face was a picture. "What's going on, *Brother*?" I deliberately emphasised the word, needing to reach him. This couldn't be happening.

He still wouldn't look me in the eye, but instead focused on a spot right behind my head. He couldn't afford to show weakness now, but nor could he look at me. "I'm sorry, this is the only way. Hands up."

I did, raising them slowly up to my ears.

Lucca reached out to open my jacket at the same time Anthony reached in and drew my own 1911n from its holster and shoved it into his belt. They didn't bother patting me down, it was common knowledge I didn't carry a second piece.

"Damn it, Turk, what are you doing?" I struggled to keep my voice, the feeling of being unarmed leaving me feeling cold and almost naked.

His eyes finally found mine. "It's an answer for your killing Tsabor. Because of your history, the Russians view it as an unprovoked revenge killing. Not business. It was personal, John."

I had to hand it to him, he said it all masterfully, with a cool steely edge to his tone that was sharper than a razor's. If I didn't know better, I could have almost sworn he was serious.

I couldn't believe what I was hearing. *Personal? They were about to gun us all down!*"

"Maybe. But they claim it was all in response to Tsabor's murder, and they say you have to answer for it. Your death will cancel out Tsabor's murder and the shooting. I'm sorry, if there had been other witnesses to survive the night and back up your claims…" He trailed off, and I hoped the lies were like bile in his mouth.

And suddenly it all made sense. The supposed abruptness of it all, the location, the timing. It was all a lie. This wasn't a meet, a show of powerplay. It was a secretly prearranged execution. My execution. I was being made a sacrifice, a sacrificial peace cow.

Twice now I had humiliated Alexi and his men. First by surviving my parents murder as a boy. Then again that night on Fifth avenue, by not only foiling his plans to seize territory from the warring families, but by killing Tsabor, crippling his organisation. I made him look weak.

He wanted his revenge.

Hell, even the last-minute changing of the guard suddenly made sense. Lucca and Anthony were the only two soldiers stupid enough to think they could point a gun at me and think they could live to tell the story.

"And what about Pa?" I pressed on, growing desperate, knowing he had no choice but to put me down. "Does my blood wash that away too?"

He stiffened at that and for one brief moment, my heart jumped. It was a cheap shot, but I didn't care.

I needed to reach him.

He sighed, and looked down. "He has already given this the go ahead." He said it like a father telling his kids there was no Santa. "I'm sorry brother I really am, but there's no other way. The Familia cannot survive another war."

"Look at me, goddamn it Turk! Look at me!" I could practically feel the cold metal of Anthony's gun metal pressing into my ear at my outburst, but I was passed caring.

I needed him to look at me. Look me in the eye.

He did. His stormy grey eyes met mine, firm and unwavering. He might not have liked it, but he was set and resolved. This was the only way. His only choice.

He needed to put the family first. Our family.

Fair enough, I understood that, but no one said *I* had to like it.

"I'm sorry," he said again and suddenly his Beretta Px4 was in his hand and levelled at me.

"Is that all you have to say?"

"It is, goodbye *brother*-"

"Tempus fugit, DeCampo. I am not renowned for my patience. Put the dog down and let us conclude our business."

You only have a moment.

Sometimes it is at the start and you miss it as the moment rushes ahead of you while your brain struggles to catch up. Sometimes people miss it because they're waiting for that perfect moment to escape.

Then sometimes it comes just when you think it's all over.

And when Turk glanced sideways towards Alexi, I didn't hesitate.

That was a preview of Reaper, Rogue Warrior Book 2, A Tarzan Retelling.

A collection of hot and orgasmic stories by The Lord of Lust

Do you love hard men, strong women, sizzling chemistry and erotic scenes that make Fifty Shades of Grey look like five shades of beige?

Well, here you go…

7 Books, 7 hard and rugged men, 7 sizzling page turners that will have you devouring every word from start to finish…

A Tropical Cocktail Boxset

Romance is in the air in this two book Holiday
Romance boxset that is all about sun, sea and sex…
Tequila Sunset
Beneath The Sheets

Alpha Men of the Otherworld

The battle of the Species is about to rage, and only the true alpha will come out on top in the Lord of Lust hottest new duo boxset that sees vampires and werewolves lock tooth and claw…

Temptation at its Sweetest…

Book 1: The Babysitter
Book 2: The Boss's Daughter

Sweet Temptations: books 1&2 are sizzling tales that break all the rules and combine lust, seduction and temptation. Loaded with drama and heat, this boxset will ignite your ereader and leave you panting for more.

To all the rest of the world, Elizabeth Clarke has it all. A successful husband. A beautiful home. And now a son off to university. She is a perfect housewife with the perfect life.

It's a lie.

Her husband is a lying, drinking philanderer who hates her as much as she loathes him. Her home is beautiful, but empty, nothing more than a gilded cage to keep her trapped in a world she never wanted.

That is, until he came back into town.

Hugh Becket.

Her son's best friend. He's hot, young, and so forbidden.

Elizabeth knows she should stay away, but when the devil comes knocking on her door in the middle of the night, what's a poor neglected trophy wife to do?

He is my Hades
I'd played the role of a goddess, bound and chained
for the service of mortals.
He freed me.
He freed me, unchained me and taken me to his
underworld, his dark realm where he'd brought out
all my forbidden and secret desires.
And now I'm his.
His attendant. His servant…

When Mina returns for her stepbrother's 21st birthday, she thinks her days of lusting after him are over. Caught up in the heat and passion of the moment, she is stunned to find them back in bed together; their feelings clearly far from resolved. Haunted by her desire, Mina now has another problem... she must head down a path of lust and desire; torn between the dark delights of the handsome bad boy down the street and her adorable stepbrother who has always been there for her. Can she confront the truth she has long tried to bury? How far will she go to save the one she wants, but knows she can never truly have?

THE LORD OF LUST
L.M. MOUNTFORD

I know it's wrong to want my best friend's dad… but what about when his wife offers to share?

Tracey has known the Burtons practically all her life.
They're her best friend's parents.
When she was a little girl they took her on days out to the beach. But she's a woman now, and they have some very important lessons to teach her…

'I'm sorry Cassy, but you're just too boring for me,'
That was the story of Cassandra's life.
She was always that girl. The curvy plain jane. She
was fine with it, right up until her hot bad boy ex
threw it in her face before walking out of her life.
Leaving her depressed and reeling, doubting
everything about herself and her future…
So her best friend has spirited her away to her
family's Gibraltar Vila for a little fun in the sun, some
much needed girl time, and a whole lot of boys.
There's just one problem.
David, her best friend's recently divorced dad also
happens to be staying at the villa. And he's no boy…

Sooner or later, the thirst always wins…

After a thousand years, Lucian had given up any interest in the world. His only concern that night was finding his next drink, preferably from a flavoursome twenty-something with loose morals and no expectations. Then he saw her…

Kate is just a girl from the country, who came to the city with her brother to find a life away from their parents' car crash. That is, until the police came knocking on her door one morning and ripped her new life apart.

Now she has nothing and no one, with only one on her mind…

When these worlds collide, and the things that go bump in the night come calling, can these two mend the rifts in each other and give them what they need?

Alex's life was circling the drain, and he was officially one step away from hitting rock bottom after finding his long-term girlfriend in bed with his biggest clients. Then one morning an email arrives from the last person on earth he ever expected to hear from again. Sarah Snow. His childhood friend, and the uncontested love of his life whom he hasn't seen since prom night. And before he could say travel agent, he was boarding the first plane bound for Sydney, Australia, with nothing but his passport and an overnight bag. He's no idea what he'll do or say when he finally reunites with the girl that broke his heart, but one thing's for sure…

He's not going home without her.